WHAT
FOLLOWS ...

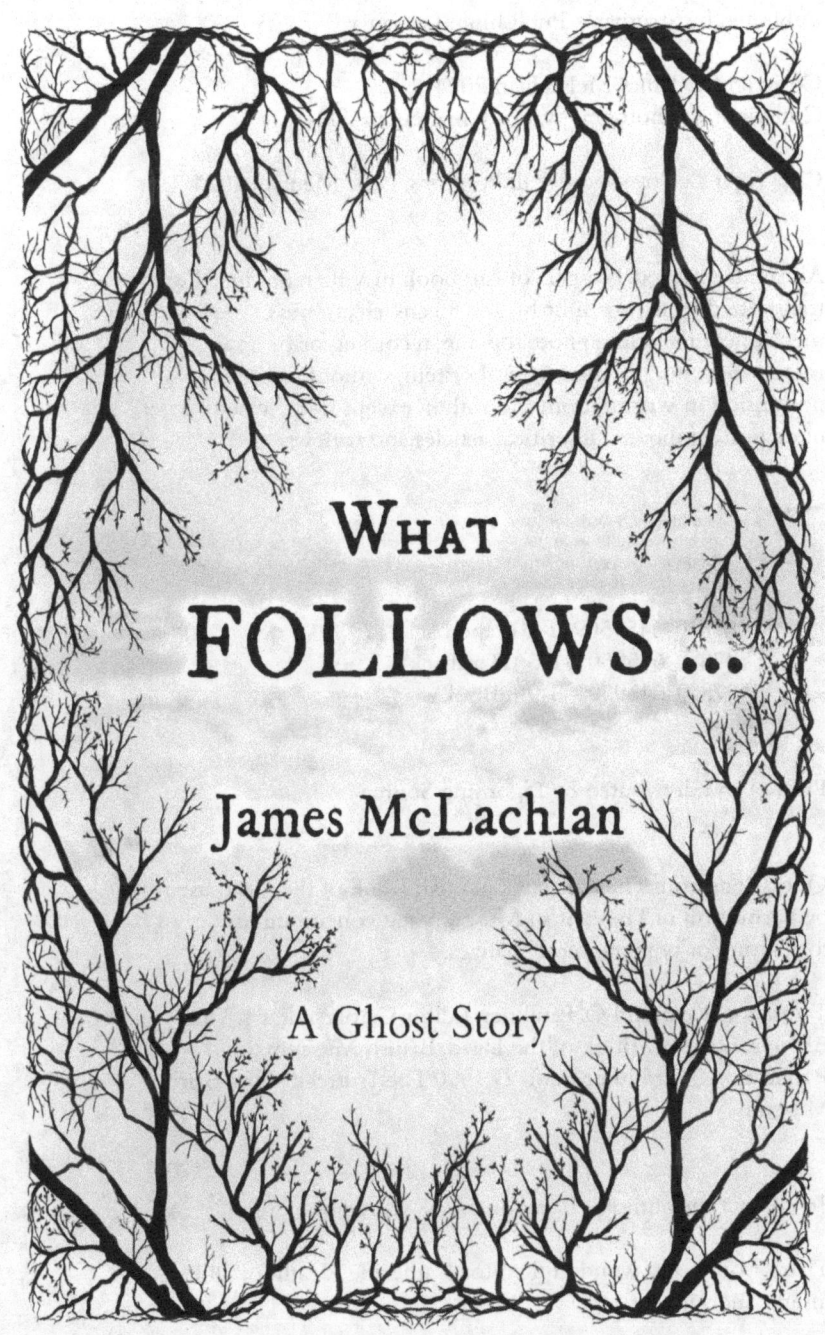

WHAT
FOLLOWS ...

James McLachlan

A Ghost Story

Sp
STRUTHARSE PUBLISHING

Published by Strutharse Publishing, Tasmania

A catalogue record for this
book is available from the
National Library of Australia

ISBN   978-0-6459509-2-2 (Paperback)
        978-0-6459509-1-5 (Hardback)
        978-0-6459509-3-9 (eBook)

Printed and distributed by Lightning Source

Quotations from The Ancient Egyptian Book of the Dead used
by permission of The British Museum and contain minor
formatting or typographical changes.

Translator Raymond O. Faulkner, Editor Carol Andrews, The
Ancient Egyptian Book of the Dead, British Museum
Publications, third impression © 1990 The Trustees of the British
Museum.

To contact the author: occasionaldross.wordpress.com

Thank you to my wonderful editor Catherine Heath for all her
insight and support.

For Julie,
knower of literary things

The Diary of Jane Hill

What follows is a record of our trip on the Overland Track, through the Cradle Mountain – Lake St Clair National Park in north-west Tasmania, as recorded by me, Jane Hill. The members of our group are Alice Northrop, Mary Bell, Yvonne Fenn and myself.

PRE-TRIP THOUGHTS

So David died. That's probably the most appropriate way to start this. It's the reason we're going on this trip. I think. It's all a bit sketchy so far. Our friend David Holt died in a climbing accident a few weeks ago. He fell, apparently only a short distance, but by some fluke it managed to kill him. I still find it hard to believe he's really gone. Alice decided we should do this long bushwalk so we aren't moping about feeling sorry for ourselves. Personally I don't think I am moping, but maybe Alice sees something I don't. I *am* upset by it. At least – I don't know. I really don't know.

I think Alice has some idea of this trip being an 'all girls together' sort of thing. But as I've watched her organising it I've found myself thinking that the rest of us – Yvonne, Mary and I – are only a peripheral detail. Maybe I'm imagining it, but sometimes it's like she only thinks of us as things she's required to pack and bring with her for the trip. I'm not sure how far I can trust my feelings – my intuition – just now, not when everything's still so raw about David. Oh, you silly boy, why did you have to go and leave us like this?

Sometimes Alice reminds me of one of those Agatha Christie characters – the ones that live on a small farm in the country, are unmarried (in the modern TV adaptions they always get turned into lesbians for some reason), and are obsessed with dogs – although I don't think Alice has ever been near a farm, and she doesn't have the space for a dog. She *is* single, however, and she's very forthright like they are, very sure of herself and her abilities. It's hard to say no to someone like Alice; she thinks all things are possible for all people. I only wish she wasn't making the rest of us do something so physical and 'outdoorsy' with her. That's far more in her line than ours. It reminds me too much of what David was doing when he died. Perhaps that's it, though; she wants us all to go and do something he'd have liked doing himself. I'm pretty sure he hadn't done the Overland Track. Now we'll do it for him. Good grief! Where did that bit of trite sentimentality come from? I'm sure Alice doesn't see it like that. I think I'm overtired.

Alice has had all this nervous energy lately, rushing around everywhere, doing this, doing that. Maybe this walk is what she needs to get the bees out of her bonnet, or whatever it is. She's hardly said anything about David since he died – just this trip, she's always on about doing this trip.

Right now I'm sorting out things to pack. As I've never been on a walk like this before, I still have a lot more stuff to buy, and it's turning out to be very expensive. The annoying thing is not knowing what I need to take. It's just about the middle of winter now, and it's going to be very cold up there. But how cold is very cold? Will I need more clothing than I can fit in my pack? How much food am I going to want to eat? Anything I don't end up using will be weight I won't have needed to carry. But what if we get snowed in? I suppose I should ask the people at the camping shop about doing this particular walk in winter the next time I go in – though they *are* trying to sell me stuff and make money, so can I really trust their advice? Maybe I can just use my ordinary clothes to do it. I can just picture my inexperience coming through and messing things up. I hope Alice knows what she's letting herself in for. *She's* the bushwalker, the mountain climber, the tally-ho horseriding one. I've asked her advice on a lot of things – when I can get her to sit still for five seconds – but I get the impression that *her* needs on a long bushwalk will be different to mine. I suppose I'll just have to wait and see what happens.

A List of Things to Pack

Based on a pretty rushed reading of the guide book and the internet, and some advice from Alice, I have compiled a rough list of the things I intend to take on the trip:

walking shoes

shoes for walking about the camp site

socks, 3 pairs

gaiters (not sure about these – but other people use them)

trousers for walking in

trousers for wearing around camp

thermal trousers

waterproof trousers

knickers, 3 pairs

sports bra for walking

comfy bra for camp

walking top

top for camp

thermal top

warm jacket

waterproof jacket, with hood

waterproof gloves

woolly hat

sun hat

sunglasses (I wonder if I'll use those!)

sunscreen

head torch

small hand torch

spare batteries (enough to last for weeks)

water bottle

water bladder (a small one I can carry when it's full! Alice says
    that should be enough)

toilet paper

toilet trowel

wet wipes

pads (just in case!)

ziplock bags

toothbrush and toothpaste

deodorant (internet says not to bother, but I will)

antibacterial hand gel

small towel

first-aid kit

pocketknife

compass (don't really know how to use one)

pens, 2

notebook – this diary

map of the Overland Track

guidebook

pack of Cards Against Humanity

waterproof matches

cooking utensils

bowl and plate

tin mug

food (pre-mixed coffee, pre-mixed porridge, chocolate, dried
    fruit and nuts, dehydrated meals, muesli bars, etc.)

sleeping bag

sleeping-bag liner

sleeping mat

walking pack

walking-pack liner

walking-pack cover (Alice says assume everything will get wet) cord for tent, etc.

small purse with money, cards etc. (will need these for each end
of the walk)

phone (no reception on the track, but take it anyway. Plus can
use as spare camera, though battery drain!)

~~spirit stove~~ (sharing Yvonne's)

~~tent~~ (sharing Yvonne's)

~~emergency beacon~~ (Alice is bringing)

~~trekking poles~~ (one more thing to carry – just find a stick!)

At the moment the Overland Track is fully booked up, as they
only let a certain number of people walk it each year. I thought this
would put an end to Alice's idea – thrilled as I was to be going during
the middle of winter, with waist-high snow to walk through – but
Alice doesn't like to be beaten, and she came up with a way to get
around this. Apparently the park closes the track down for a week
every year, and this is due to happen again in about a week's time.
Alice wants us to sneak onto the track and walk it while it's closed.
They close it down, apparently, because winter is normally when the
worst weather hits – and it also saves money on rangers and things. I
don't know what they'll do if they catch us there; simply kicking us
out is hardly a threat, as the only way to get out is to walk out, which
means we'll have finished doing the track anyway. It's either that or
fly us out in a helicopter, and I can't see them spending money on
helicopter fuel just for that. Alice thinks it'll be easy to sneak in

somewhere because the park covers such a large area (1,614 km^2) and, once we're on the track, there'll be no rangers around to see us. This sounds logical, but the last thing I want to have to do is walk the last 40 km in shame, knowing I'm going to meet more angry rangers at the end, and have to pay a huge fine or whatever it is that happens.

But my main worry in travelling through the middle of the coldest, most weather-racked part of the year, with its hypothermia-inducing snow and wind, is that should our group get into any kind of trouble (and only one of us has had any real bushwalking experience), there won't be the usual nearby help on the track to stop us from dying. Alice, ever the optimist, says this won't be a problem – on such a long walk as this, if we got into so much trouble that we were in danger of dying, we'd probably succumb to it before we could find help anyway, even if the place was crawling with rangers. Great. I suppose there's a logic to this as well – sort of – and Alice knows what she's doing. Plus there's the safety-in-numbers thing. And it will keep Alice happy.

We'll be saving money too. If we wait until some places become available, the weather will get better, and there's a fee to walk the track during the most popular part of the year – which is fair enough, as the track and facilities have to be maintained and the rangers need paying for looking after everybody. Alice says this is the best time of year to go in that respect. And I must admit there's a part of me that finds it hard to have to pay to do something that involves such a tremendous amount of physical exertion on my part. It's odd to say, but it feels like they should be paying *us* for doing it! What's more, before you cough up for the privilege of doing the walk, you first need to pay to get into the national park to be able to get to the start of the thing. It's like you're paying twice. Sneaking onto the track will mean we might not have to pay for that, either. I do feel a little guilty about this, but it can't be helped if we're to follow Alice's plan. I think I'll send in a donation when we get back from the trip.

What we *do* have to pay for is transportation to the start of the track at Cradle Mountain, and then back again from the Lake St Clair visitor centre at the finish. We'll also need someone to drive us so they can take the car away with them. Then there are all the things we've had to buy to take with us, like tents, sleeping bags, clothes, food and all that sort of stuff. I've already bought some of mine, but I'm still umming and ahing about a lot of things. Will I need them or won't I? And can I get them cheaper from another shop? It's all been such a rush.

Some Facts about the Overland Track

The Overland Track is 65, 70, 73, 74, 79 or 80 km long,
depending on which guidebook or website you consult.

It takes five, six or seven days to complete – weather permitting.

It is walked by about 2,000 people each year.

The area became a national park in 1971.

It includes Tasmania's tallest peak (Mount Ossa at 1,617 m).

It has Australia's deepest lake (Lake St Clair at 160, 200 or
215 m, again depending on the source you use).

You have to take your used tampons and pads out with you.

There is no soap or detergent allowed, even the special biodegradable stuff.

There are no camp fires allowed.

There are wombats, possums, Tasmanian devils, pademelons and a heap of unique plants I'm sure I won't notice.

It is important to tell people where you're going and how long you plan your trip to take, as a search will only be conducted if someone reports you missing. Oh dear.

Pre-Trip Thoughts Continued

It's been a blurred rush this past week. Now that the dust has settled a little after getting all my gear together and organising time off work, it's finally dawned on me that we really are going to do this. We really are going to do this walk – we're leaving tomorrow. The thing is, I don't actually recall saying yes to going. It's Alice that's been pushing to make this trip happen. The rest of us have just been pulled along in the wake of her enthusiasm. I forget that Alice can be like this sometimes. You know she doesn't concern herself with what you might think about something, but you let her get on with things her way all the same. Perhaps that's why it's taken this long for me to ask myself why I'm going on this walk. I confronted her about it, and she said that David had wanted us all to do it together, so that's why we're going. What could I say to that? I have to go now; I'm not going to be the only one left out and be made to feel guilty about it by the others. And it's not that I don't want to go, or be involved; I just don't understand why we have to do something so epic. Of course, I realise I might just be being lazy,

and I'm feeling a little vulnerable right now, which I think is understandable, so I'm uncertain of my feelings. It's just that it seems like this is going to be a week-long wake, this trip. Is that morbid? I'm pretty sure Mary feels this way. I haven't seen her much since David's funeral, and I think she's been spending a lot of time on her own. I'm not even sure if she'll turn up for the trip, but Alice said she's coming.

Anyway, I've rambled on enough here. I don't wish to sound pessimistic and, on the whole, I do have a good feeling about this walk. The actual walking bit will probably start to drive me bonkers after a few days, but by the end of it – when we're all knackered – I suppose we'll be glad we did it.

Day One

In the Car

We're on our way.

Our friend Liz Gore is driving us to Cradle Mountain and will pick us up from the other end when we've finished. The plan is for her to drop us off just outside the park so we can sneak in while she drives through the tollgate with our packs hidden in the back of her car. This is so the person on the gate won't see a carload of people going into the park, but only one person leaving it. Then she'll pick us up again from somewhere inside and drive us to the start of the walk. It's going to take us six days to do comfortably so, to be on the safe side, Liz is going to meet us the day after at the Lake St Clair visitor centre in Cynthia Bay. Of course, if the weather turns bad and we fall more than a day behind schedule she'll have to wait for us, which I can't imagine will be much fun. So a big thank you to Liz for doing that.

But will it really be that easy to sneak in? I keep wondering if the parks people might have set up something that Alice hasn't thought of to stop people getting onto the track. It feels like a lot of trouble we're going to, just so we can do the walk now rather than wait for some places to become available next year, even if we are saving money. But Alice wants to go now and she's organised everything. Alice is *always* organising everything. It also seems pointless to close the track for only one week; I can't think how it saves them much money in rangers' wages and such.

Evening – near Waterfall Valley Hut

Here we are – our first evening on the track. It's hard to believe we're actually here.

We've pitched and hidden our tents in the bush near the camping site for Waterfall Valley Hut – Yvonne and me in one, Alice and Mary in the other – so anyone coming along won't see us, and Alice has brought two green coverings, which we've stretched over them for camouflage. It's a pity we have to go to such lengths, especially as the real camp site is so nice, but as we aren't supposed to be here it seems best not to flaunt our presence. If there is anyone about on the track – maintenance workers, etc. – they'll be bound to come to the huts and camping sites.

At the moment we're sitting on a helicopter pad, watching the sun go down – everything needed to maintain the track has to be helicoptered in and out of the park. It's chilly but the sky is clear and the view is beautiful. It would be wonderful if the weather could stay like this for the whole trip, but the forecast is for snow in the next few days, though the weather is hard to predict around here, apparently. Still, a wonderful start. Everyone content.

When we arrived at the national park, we drove up and down for a bit until we found somewhere we thought we could get in without being seen. This we eventually did, but then had to play a long game of hide-and-seek as we tried to find Liz and the car on the other side. Then, after a quick drive around, we went and had a look at the information centre. There was snow on the sides of the road everywhere, but nothing new could have fallen for several days.

Finally, we drove out to the Ronny Creek car park where the Overland Track officially starts – or finishes, depending on which way around you do it. There's a little hut there where you register your walk so the rangers know you're on the track. We didn't, obviously, and leaving this behind reminded me that there's going to be no one on the track to help us if we get into trouble. Are we being irresponsible? Why is Alice always in such a hurry to do things? She says we'll be fine. And people do the walk by themselves all the time, even in the winter. They write about it on the internet. Hardly anyone ever gets into trouble – statistically. It's too late to go back now, anyway. And I'm not going to be the one to let the others down. Yvonne actually likes the thought of having the run of the place.

'Why would you want to do a walk in the bush if you know you're going to be bumping into people all the time?' she said.

I take her point. Sort of. At least Liz knows where we've gone and expects us back at a certain time. I think I'm just overreacting.

Today's leg was from the Ronny Creek car park to Waterfall Valley Hut. The guidebook says it's 10.4 km and takes about five hours to walk, but I didn't keep track of how long it took us to do. The first section was along a raised wooden walkway that the guidebook calls 'duckboards', with chicken wire nailed to it. Snaking its way across the green and brown grasses into the low-hanging morning mist, it made the going very easy. The landscape was open and mostly flat with an occasional bush or small tree to break things up. Then we crossed Ronny Creek Bridge and climbed into a forest, following the creek with its many offshoots, and passed Crater Falls. This was a very good place for taking photos.

Next we came to Crater Lake and the old boatshed, where we stopped to rest. I presume everyone who does the walk stops here; it's certainly the right sort of place for it. The lake is a 'cirque' (a hollow carved out by a glacier) and its water is very clear – though tending to be a little tea coloured – and very calm. I've seen pictures of the lake and the boatshed before. They use a lot of shots taken from here to advertise the walk. I presume it's been a long while since anyone's taken a boat out on the lake. Everything in the park is supposed to remain in its natural state, apart from the upkeep of the sleeping huts. The rangers aren't even allowed to tidy up the fallen tree branches, so the animals and insects can use them as they rot. There are also no fires allowed in the park, no throwing out food waste – so no feeding the animals, directly or indirectly. It makes me feel like we aren't walking through real bush at all. It's like we're in a 'nature' theme park; you can't do anything 'bushy' here.

Leaving the boatshed, we followed the track up to a ridge, where there's a lookout with lake views on both sides. It was very misty when we were up there, but still lots to see. The air tasted wonderfully clean, and I kept taking huge gulps of it.

And now we come to the climb up to Marions Lookout on the edge of Cradle Plateau. It was a short climb, but it nearly killed us – going almost straight up at one point – and we had to haul our heavy packs up with us. I was so exhausted when I finally reached the top that I had to lie down, although 'fell down' would be a better description. This left me stranded on my back because of my huge pack, like an upside-down tortoise. I unclipped myself and managed to roll over and get my jacket off, but after only a few minutes the cold wind up there chilled the sweat on my body and I had to put it back on again. This is turning out to be a problem: the amount of clothing we need to wear to keep warm while we're standing still becomes stifling when we're walking, so we have to wear less but keep on moving.

And what could we see from Marions Lookout after all this? Mist. Mist and more mist. Mist everywhere – we were right inside it. No wonder I started feeling so cold. The guidebook says we should have gotten our first proper look at Cradle Mountain from here, with Dove Lake below. It was very isolating and dreamy amongst all that mist as well – four little people on that big mountain, like there were no other human beings anywhere in the world. Cold and silent.

From here we headed south-west for 1.5 km (according to the guidebook) along more duckboard walkways across the plateau, which was covered in short vegetation and a lot of tarns (small mountain lakes) filled with clear water. The mist disappeared – mostly – opening up a blue sky, and we saw Barn Bluff and then got our first look at Cradle Mountain (1,545 m). Cradle Mountain is supposedly named after a child's cradle, but I don't see it myself.

Ten minutes more and we came to Kitchen Hut, where we stopped to have lunch. It's a two-storey hut with an entrance on each level – presumably in case it snows up to the second level – and is only used in emergencies. For lunch I had a small tin of tuna (which did need to be drained before I could eat it, so I hope I haven't killed anything with the brine) and two packets of sultanas mixed with bits of dried pineapple. It's an impressive spot, an enormous open space with mountains all around. I felt like an ant walking through it.

I remember it was about here that Yvonne said something along the lines of 'It's lovely here today, even though it's winter. And we've got it all to ourselves. But I don't understand what the problem is; why have they closed the track?'

'They can't afford to pay the staff all year round,' said Alice. 'Everyone's broke these days.'

'Well, yeah ... but only for a week? Why would you bother to close it at all? And they'd have to turn down track fees while it's closed.'

Alice stood up. 'I don't know,' she said. 'There might be nice weather right now, but it *is* the middle of winter. Perhaps people don't want to do it at this time of year.'

'But it's always booked out, isn't it?' said Yvonne. 'People have to wait to do it because they only allow a certain number through each year.'

'There you are, then,' said Alice. 'They do it to keep the numbers down.'

'Maybe they do maintenance for a week,' suggested Mary. 'Or something like that. Perhaps they clean the huts, and they don't want people in them while they're doing it.'

This wasn't a welcome thought. We don't want the camp sites to be full of workmen when we're trying to go through unseen.

'I don't think so,' said Alice. 'The woman I spoke to at Parks and Wildlife was certain the whole track gets closed off for the week.'

'It still seems strange to me,' said Yvonne.

It *is* a bit odd, so I hope the Parks and Wildlife woman is right. I don't want any surprises popping up.

We finished our lunch and left Kitchen Hut behind, walking the short distance to the next track junction, which takes you up Cradle Mountain – though none of us could be bothered doing the detour to go up it – and then headed south for 1.2 km, following a series of ridges below the western slopes of the mountain. We had to negotiate several large muddy puddles as we went. In fact, some parts of the track were just water-filled trenches with rocks at the bottom of them. We could step over some of these, as there were protruding rocks, but others we had no choice but to wade through. The Parks and Wildlife people don't like you to go around, as it widens the track. I didn't mind getting my feet wet, as Alice had already warned us that it was inevitable on a walk like this. And it took a surprising amount of time for the water to leak through my boots.

Passing through patches of light forest, we then crossed a small creek at the head of Fury River and continued along the rocky track for another kilometre or so, rising onto Cradle Cirque and a junction leading to Lake Rodway, where we took some photos of the impressive Barn Bluff (1,559 m). Again, it looked more like a big lump of rock than a barn to me. There was another junction 700 m further on, going up Barn Bluff, where we stopped for a rest and took a few more photos. I got some shots of Benson Peak and Cradle Mountain in the distance. We then turned left to the south-east towards Waterfall Valley, where – apparently – you can see a lot of waterfalls after it's been raining.

From here the track descended steeply to the south-west through a eucalypt forest and into Waterfall Valley. At a further junction we turned right and followed the signposts to Waterfall Valley Hut, which sleeps twenty-four people, and then onto an older hut 100 m further along, which sleeps eight. Not far from here are the camp sites. There is also a water tank and composting toilets. The toilets are perched on stilts to allow the waste to drop down into big round fiberglass containers, which are shipped out by helicopter when full.

It's been a long day. We've walked over 10 km. The others went back to the camp site to cook dinner a while ago, so Yvonne should have finished with our stove by now. It's been nice sitting here writing in the sun – very peaceful and completely quiet. The sun is just starting to go down. Time for dinner.

Day Two

Afternoon – Windermere Hut

We woke this morning to find the weather had changed. It was raining heavily and I think it had been doing so for most of the night. I'd left my walking boots outside to dry, so they were soaked when I put them on, but it wasn't really a problem, as they got wet when I started to walk in them anyway. This was more the sort of weather I'd been expecting us to encounter. Still, it's not snowing yet.

Cooking breakfast was cramped. Yvonne and I took it in turns to squat in the doorway of our tent, cooking on Yvonne's little spirit stove set up in the vestibule. I had my porridge mix with some bits of dried fruit thrown in, and then we boiled water for coffee. But to get the water, clean the cooking things and pack the tents up, there was nothing for it but to put on our raincoats and waterproof pants,

go outside and get drenched. As Alice had said, there's no point in being too precious about it.

Today's trek was shorter than yesterday's – about 7 km – so we didn't have to hurry off, but we thought that the earlier we started the earlier we'd reach the next hut: Windermere.

It didn't look like the rain was going to let up anytime soon, so we set off and covered the short distance back onto the main track. Here we turned right and walked for about 2 km along duckboards and boggy paths through a rain-drenched landscape of open dark green and sort of yellow-green forest. The going was more difficult on today's walk. Some of the duckboards merely consisted of pairs of planks set lengthways, which meant that we had to walk in single file and couldn't change our positions without fear of falling into the vegetation or mud. This would be easy to do in the slippery snow, or when put off balance by our heavy packs.

Eventually we reached a soggy junction, in what felt like the middle of nowhere, leading to Lake Will, and we stopped to rest. We didn't sit down while we were here because of the wet, but we'd also gotten sick of taking off our packs and putting them back on every time we stopped anywhere. But, despite this, I don't think any of us were that put out by walking in the terrible weather. Well, maybe Mary. This is what a proper bushwalk is supposed to be like. And we were all wearing our fancy waterproof things, which have kept us wonderfully dry so far.

Possibly because of this, we decided to do the side trip to Lake Will and Innes Falls. Ironically, the guidebook says it is a recommended trip in fine weather. But it was flat and easy going, and only took us about an hour each way. I took a few photos, and it was strange to be setting foot on a sandy beach so far from the sea.

Then it was back to the junction and another 1.5 km, the track rising to the top of a high ridge, from which we could see Mount

Pelion East and Mount Ossa – with Mount Pelion West and others behind them. From here it quickly descended and we headed south for another kilometre, coming to the south-west corner of Lake Windermere. Even though today's walk was a shorter distance than we covered yesterday, the side trip to Lake Will had brought it up to about the same walking time, and yesterday's effort was catching up with me just then. All the way down the rocky track I was looking and looking out for a glimpse of the next hut. I began to think it would never appear.

I somehow became separated from the others for most of this section, and I wasn't sure if they were behind or in front of me. It would have been a fine thing to end up doing the rest of the walk separately, and only meeting up right at the end! After I had failed to catch them up, or they failed to catch *me* up, I admit I did start to feel a little anxious about being separated, especially given our situation. But this didn't last long. We were all on the same track, so logically we would all end up at Windermere Hut together.

Why I'd got it into my head that the finish lay directly at the bottom of this section, I don't know, because we (or just I at that moment) then headed away from the lake through a valley of buttongrass rising to the south-east (the guidebook says it's buttongrass). Here I managed to get back some of my lost wind. Then – finally – I got to the hut and found the others. I should sleep well tonight.

Windermere Hut is hidden on the edge of a myrtle forest and, as we haven't seen any signs of people being about, Alice has decided we can risk staying inside it tonight. I wasn't sure about this myself, but everyone else has sided with Alice, so I didn't raise any objection. We are two days walk into the track, after all, and it's giving us a chance to dry out our wet things, especially the tents. The hut is a modern building, in good repair, and made of wooden planking with

a corrugated-iron roof. It is divided into two rooms. The first is a long sort of living room filled with steel-topped tables and benches for cooking on, and the second has sixteen wooden bunks for sleeping. I was surprised to see it has gas heating, but Alice thinks this is probably more for drying clothes than for heating the room. We're only going to use it for that purpose, but it will keep us warm at the same time. It has a lot of windows and, as the sun hasn't gone down, we can look right into the trees outside, but there are no other amenities inside. Water comes from a tank outside, and there are toilets.

It had continued to rain for another few hours after we set off from Waterfall Valley Hut, so we felt rather sweaty and soggy from walking in our jackets all day. Mary wanted to have a shower! In fact, I almost think she expected the huts to be equipped with them. She might get a shock when she goes to use the composting toilets! I was worried these wouldn't be operational, since the track is closed, but I had a quick look earlier and they – or at least the ones they have at this hut – are fine. Smelly, but fine. They have a bin of rice husks with a little cup on a string so you can cover what you drop down with something absorbent. Anyway, simply getting into some dry clothes has made me feel a lot better. I'm glad I bought a pack cover and pack liner to make sure everything stays dry. It feels strange to be using these public facilities when we're the only four people here. I've been thinking of those 'after the apocalypse' type movies where there's the last person left on earth, or someone wakes up to find the whole city has been evacuated without them. They find themselves a car to drive around in and change it for another when the petrol gets used up, and get their food from supermarkets and shops, just walking through them taking whatever they need, or going to the big department stores and riding the bikes in the toy department and picking out clothes from endless racks of the same thing. Living like that must be strange. There's nothing wrong with what you're doing – there's only yourself and your survival to consider, as it's just you among the decaying ruins of a recently extinct civilisation – but there must still be a sense that you're very wrong to be taking advantage of the situation, abusing a space that was never designed to be used without the regular social constraints.

Right now we're cooking. It's early to be having dinner, but it's giving us something to do. Alice and Mary are cooking something together, and Yvonne is making *chana masala* for the both of us while I write this. She's better at using the stove than I am. Again, I feel spoilt, as we have the whole hut to ourselves. It must be cramped when this place is full of people. But the luxury of the space serves to magnify their absence. The silence of the bush outside comes through, filling up any space we don't use, and I can feel something of what it must be like when there are no people here at all: an ancient feeling, known only to animals. It can be felt floating in from the other room where the sleeping berths are. Outside is vast and empty. The trees and bushes surrounding the hut mean nothing; they are part of the emptiness, and can do nothing to hide us. I catch Mary looking out of the window from time to time. I know she's worried about rangers finding us here, but it's as if she's also keeping an eye on the 'out there' as well. I've caught myself glancing at the window, too. When we were out there walking in it we were a part of it; now that we're here in the hut – an unnatural space built by humans – the bush has become some sort of 'other' or 'thing' surrounding us, capable of protecting or crushing us with its vast bulk. It's really hitting me that we four are the only people for a long, long way around.

Night

When it got dark outside we started playing Cards Against Humanity by the light of our head torches while eating chocolate and nuts. Anyone else who might be on the track with us would have stopped walking by then, so it was unlikely they'd turn up to discover us. We were feeling more relaxed and enjoying being out of the weather.

For some reason, Yvonne has brought along a copy of *The Ancient Egyptian Book of the Dead* and has been sporadically reading excerpts to us. I've got it with me now, so I can quote from it verbatim – Yvonne has dog-eared all the pages she has read from. For example, the 'Spell for repelling a beetle':

> Begone from me, O Crooked-lips! I am Khnum, Lord
> of Peshnu, who despatches the words of the gods to
> Re, and I report affairs to their master.

It's funny how different cultures do death. Is that the right word: 'funny'? Maybe I mean 'interesting'. It's interesting how we commemorate/celebrate dying and what comes after. I think it's because of David that Yvonne's thoughts have turned to the metaphysical. I've noticed no one has mentioned him since we started the walk. I suppose that's why we're doing it, really, so we don't have to. We aren't ready.

'Here's another one,' said Yvonne, '"Another spell for a man's going out into the day against his foes in the realm of the dead".'

> I have dug up the sky, I have hacked up the horizon, I
> have traversed the earth to its furthest extent, I have
> taken possession of the spirits of the great ones, because
> I am one who equips a myriad with my magic. I eat

with my mouth, I defecate with my hinder-parts, for I
am a god, lord of the Netherworld.

Poor David's funeral was pretty simple in comparison to what the
ancient Egyptians were into. We just stuck him in a box and put the
box in a hole in the ground. As I wasn't family or anything I didn't
get to see the body, so couldn't even swear he was really in there. All
Mary, Yvonne and I saw was a coffin lowered into a hole (Alice didn't
go). If anything actually happens after we die, if anyone even *thinks*
anything happens, it wasn't represented at the funeral. There was only
what we know, what we can be sure of. But I suppose it would be
lying to ourselves to do anything more. If he does happen to get
annoyed by a beetle, David will just have to hope for the best.

And another thing: why is it that only close family members get
to see the body, or go into the hospital room? Someone signs a bit of
paper somewhere along the line and that supposedly trumps years of
deep friendship? Even deep love?

'Oh, listen to this one,' said Yvonne. '"Spell for preventing a man's
corpse from putrefying in the realm of the dead in order to rescue
him from the eater of souls who imprisons in the Netherworld and
to prevent accusations of his crimes upon earth being imputed to
him; to cause his flesh and bones to be safe from maggots and every
god who mutilates in the realm of the dead and to allow him to
come and go as he wants and to do everything which is in his heart
without being restrained".'

That's all very well for the dead, but the living want a spell to
bring the dead back to life, surely. I wish I could bring the dead back.
There's been no mention of how to do it in the book so far. If there
is such a thing, it *would* be in something called *The Book of the Dead*.
Mind you, if you could bring the dead back to life, then there'd be
no need for all those spells to recite over them.

'Do we have to listen to this?' said Alice. She didn't attempt to mask her disdain for what Yvonne evidently thought was entertaining for us.

'But surely you want to know the "Spell for repelling two Songstress-snakes"?' said Yvonne, and she recited:

> Hail to you, you two companions, sisters, Songstresses!
> I have divided you with my magic, for I am he who
> shines in the Night-bark, I am Horus, son of Isis, and I
> have come to see my father Osiris.

Mary laughed.

'It does all seem unnecessarily complicated,' said Yvonne. 'What do you guys want for your funerals?'

'Ugh.' Mary shuddered. 'I don't want to think about it.'

'You don't care what they do with you?'

'It's morbid. I don't even want to have to arrange things for someone else's.'

'What about the *way* in which you die? You've got to have an opinion on that.'

Mary pulled a face.

'I want something spectacular and noteworthy,' said Yvonne. 'Like surfboarding into the sun while fighting a clown. What about you, Alice?'

Alice started shuffling the cards. Questions like this don't bother her.

'Something to the point with no nonsense,' she said flatly. 'With a little warning it was going to happen, preferably. Though we seldom get what we want.' She paused for a moment, then said, more quietly, 'But, whatever it is, it ought to be deserved – no more, no less than fits how we have lived and conducted ourselves. That's what would be fair.'

I've never known Alice to be religious or fatalistic before, but I can picture her there, stood in front of Death, maybe halfway up some rock face somewhere, arguing with it about whether her time has come or not. Or she might just ignore it, hoping it'll go away.

'I'm going to bed if this is what the conversation is going to be like,' announced Mary.

It's time for me to do the same. It's another long trek tomorrow, the longest of the walk – 14.2 km. We will need to keep an eye on how long it's taking us; we don't want to run out of daylight before we get to Pelion Hut.

DAY THREE

Afternoon – near Pelion Hut

Today it was the Windermere to Pelion Hut section. The guidebook says that's six hours of walking! Although the actual sign on the track says it only takes five. I suppose it depends on how fast you walk. In our case I wouldn't have thought very fast, but we made it in plenty of time before the sun started to go down. Strangely, I don't feel exhausted. I'm tired, certainly, but pleasantly so. The others seem to be in a similar sort of mood.

Our days have begun to take on something of a routine. Arriving at the next hut in the afternoon, we scout around for a place to pitch the tents, set them up, get out of our wet and muddy walking clothes into dry things, set up our sleeping things, and then – depending on the time of day – cook dinner. It's becoming automatic, with no one having to say anything about it. And when all that's done there's only a little time to fill in before we go to bed so we can get up the next

day and do it all over again. Our time is taken up with walking, eating and sleeping. I hope I'm remembering some of the things we've passed on the track, because it feels like I don't have time to take notice and enjoy them; we're always thinking about the next bit that's coming up and pushing on. I suppose that's just the way it is on a trip like this. And I don't really relish getting left behind again. I think that annoyed me more than I realised yesterday. If only you could go through the scenery without having to make so much of an effort. That way you'd have the time – and the energy – to be able to look around you more. Maybe they could build a cable car over the track, so you could sit in nice little cabins and watch the scenery go by. Perhaps with some stops so you could get out and take photos.

Changing out of our walking clothes when Yvonne and I are sharing a tent is a bit of a logistics problem too, especially if our things are wet. We've been taking it in turns to go in and get ourselves sorted, doing most of it lying down. First you take off your waterproof jacket and trousers and ball them up in the tent's vestibule, and then quickly sit down in the doorway with your feet still outside. Then you take your boots off and pull your legs into the tent. I suppose I could just do it out in the open, as there's no one here but us, and it isn't raining right now, but today I think I'll take my pack and change in the toilet after the tents have been pitched. I presume a lot of people do that trick when the camp is full and privacy is at a premium.

Leaving Windermere Hut, we got back onto the track and headed south-east across several plains from which we could see the north side of Barn Bluff. It started raining, but we soon entered the shelter of the first of several small forests. Then it was south, crossing a creek flowing from Lake Curran, and south-east to Pine Forest Moor. To the south we could see the big cliffs of Mount Pelion West, with

Mount Ossa, Mount Pelion East and Mount Oakleigh close by. Everything was wet.

Passing more tarns, we came to another track junction leading to the River Forth Lookout. We carried on, going south-east into another forest above Pine Forest Moor, and continued for about a kilometre until we emerged onto moorland, which itself stretched for a further kilometre, in the course of which we crossed two more creeks. Then, descending through another stretch of forest, we crossed Pelion Creek, where we came to (as the guidebook has it) a 'pleasant, sheltered resting place'. We rested here. We rested pleasantly – even though everything was wet and we couldn't sit down again.

Moving on (always moving on), we continued up into a forest of eucalypt, tea-tree and myrtle trees around the side of Mount Pelion West. There were a lot of waterfalls running swollen from all the rain. As we passed through the forest, small clumps of old snow lay at the foot of some of the trees, reminding us of the weather that's to come. We came to a big tree that had fallen across the track, and into which steps had been cut so we could simply walk over it. The track then descended gradually to the south for 2.5 km to Frog Flats, which was even wetter, with puddles of water everywhere. I don't know about the others but I didn't come across any frogs. There was nothing but water and silent trees.

Next we went east, crossing the flats and a bridge spanning the Forth River. I remember there was a sign for the river nailed to a tree there. This spot is also the lowest point on the Overland Track – 720 m above sea level.

I feel it only right to point out at this juncture that all this directional and measurement information comes courtesy of my guidebook, which I consult when I'm writing everything down at the end of the day. I wouldn't want any future readers to get the impression that I'm some sort of navigational prodigy. When I'm on

the track I'm just following the path, the odd signpost and Alice, who is almost always taking the lead. This doesn't bother me, as I think it would spoil the walk to know every feature that is about to come up. Alice always takes a look at the map in the mornings, so she would know if we went seriously wrong. But with the track to follow we don't really need to know where we are. So many people make this trip every year and hardly anyone ever gets lost.

I'm finding that my mind tends to go blank when I'm walking along too. It's as if all my energy is directed into the act of walking and not tripping over things or tipping over with my pack, so I don't have time for it. I just switch off, and only notice that time has passed when I come to myself again. I don't even think about David; it's as if there isn't time for it. Or maybe I'm just using that as an excuse to push those thoughts away. It's only during the night – normally when I'm trying to fall asleep and my mind is alone, without outside distractions – that thoughts of David come to me. But why should I want to push them away, other than that they make me feel sad because it's something I've lost and will never have again? I suppose it's just the thought of death – one day it will come for me as it did for David. I wonder if the others are experiencing a similar phenomenon. We don't talk very much when we're walking.

We then turned north-east and left the flats with their hidden frogs behind, climbing into another forest and continuing along for 1.2 km onto a ridge, before turning east for about another 1.6 km and arriving at the junction for Old Pelion Hut. It's only used in emergencies now, and we didn't bother going to have a look at it.

A final ten minutes or so more brought us to another junction and the tent platforms of New Pelion Hut. We've had a look and it's a large wooden building on stilts with a verandah all around, sleeping sixty. There didn't seem to be anyone about, but Alice thinks it best if we stick to the tents again for tonight, as there are several other walking tracks branching off the main track at this point, so there's more chance of someone turning up here. We've found somewhere to pitch the tents where they shouldn't be too visible, and we're again going to use Alice's camouflaged coverings.

Mine and Yvonne's is nearly up. Yvonne has been swearing at it, trying to thread the poles into the sleeves, while I've been scribbling all this down. I've had to remind her that, as 'trip recordist', I've probably been working harder than she has.

'And,' I added, 'Alice didn't have any trouble putting hers and Mary's up.' But Yvonne doesn't seem to have appreciated my encouragement. Well, her loss.

It's dinnertime now and I have a strong craving for some of the dehydrated scrambled eggs I've brought along. I've been fantasising about them all day. I wonder if I'll lose some weight doing this walk. I'll have to, surely.

Day Four

Morning

Snow! Lots of snow. It's as if someone came by in the night and iced over the landscape with white frosting. The scenery is unrecognisable. It's lucky there are signposts to tell us where to go on the track; I don't think we'd know which way to head off in otherwise. And it's still snowing.

Time to get up and have a better look around.

Later

At the moment we seem to just be hanging about, wondering what the weather is going to do. We're worried if we set off now it'll get worse and we'll be caught in it. Though I suppose we can always make camp somewhere if things get too bad. I think Alice is keen to set off today so we keep to schedule. It's a pity we don't have a way

to find out what the weather is going to be doing from day to day. Alice just tried for a phone signal but, of course, there isn't one. And the weather can change so quickly out here, anyway.

Later Still

We've decided to push on. The snow's only falling lightly, so I think we'll be all right. Time to pack up and get going. Need to dig out the thermal undies!

Afternoon – Kia Ora Hut

We've made it. And what a trek!

We're now at Kia Ora Hut and it's still snowing, but only lightly.

I think this is my favourite hut so far. It's one of the smaller ones, with everything crammed together in just one room. Half of the space has tables for cooking etc., and the other part has four shared bunks, which will sleep twenty-four people. The guidebook says it was built in 1990, so I suppose there must have been an older hut on the same site. It feels very cosy and welcoming here, even though it's surrounded by mountains and is cold like everywhere else. The exhaustion and strain, the overheating and icy blasts of wind – all that was on the track; it already seems like a distant memory now. I only feel pleasantly tired, liquescent like I'm in a dream. I think this has something to do with the hut coming at the end of such a long, wet and emotionally draining day – it feels wonderful to have reached any of the huts at all, and we've decided to stay here rather than out in the tents. There's been no sign of anyone since we left Cradle Mountain, so we should be okay to stay in a hut again.

We're on the verandah right now – some of us standing, some sitting – drinking coffee and watching the snow fall. Everything's covered in snow, with just a drab black/brown poking through here and there and a grey sky. It's very peaceful and pleasant now, but I was getting quite worried for a time earlier on. I suppose I was overreacting – no one else has said anything about it having had such an effect on them. It must have been the knowledge that we're here on our own raising its ugly head again. More about that in a minute.

We left Pelion Hut in all our wet-weather things in the falling snow and made our way back onto the main track, then headed south through forest for 1.7 km along Douglas Creek on more of those duckboards, and crossed a bridge over Sharers Hut Creek. We then climbed for 1.4 km through patches of sometimes very beautiful myrtle and eucalypt trees.

When we were nearly through this forest we came across a little memorial plaque nailed to a tree. It was for a walker who had died on the track. I can't remember the exact wording of the plaque, only that, strangely, it didn't give their name. It was just 'To the walker who died ...' etc. What was the point of a plaque without a name? But I suppose that sort of thing will happen on such a long and well-used track – people dying – and it's another reminder of what can happen to the unwary in this isolated place. It didn't say *how* they died, either.

We all paused to read this and, naturally, it made me think of David. I wondered if we should do something similar for where *he* died – put up a little memorial. It would only need to be something small and subtle like that, only with his name on it. I've been thinking of asking the others about it, but it still doesn't feel right to be bringing David up openly in the conversation. There's an awkwardness about us that I'm sure is caused by his absence and, although I don't think I'm ready for this to be challenged yet myself, with so much going on inside my head it makes me think that I'm eventually going to blurt out something by accident. I'm surprised that Yvonne hasn't said anything about David on this trip; she's the

sort of person who usually likes to talk about everything. Perhaps she doesn't want to upset us any more than we already are at the moment; perhaps she too feels this awkwardness, this ... fear we all have. Why do I use that word – 'fear'? Why should we be afraid? Is it because of our inability to speak on the matter? Or how it might affect each of us if we did? I don't understand it, but that word is there just the same. And I know it will all come out sometime, for I am certain that the others are thinking about him just as much and, once the dam does burst, then the healing can begin. Hopefully.

Whilst on the track, however, my mind continues to remain empty of almost everything except walking, walking, walking. Being here, alone in the bush, it feels as though we've left the real world behind. Maybe it's the effect of burning so much energy so suddenly, but it's almost like a dream at times. Intellectually I know time is passing – the sun comes up and goes down, and the mountains and trees slowly change – but in another sense nothing is moving here at all. It's always trees and rocks and sky – always Alice, Yvonne and Mary. There are no people coming and going, and we haven't seen any animals. I thought we'd have seen *something* by now. I suppose Tasmanian animals mostly come out at night when they can't be seen. And, even if we were doing the walk when the track was open and there were other people about, they too would come and go like the trees and the mornings – another one would be along soon, with no appreciable difference from the last. It feels like we could go on like this forever. I really miss David.

Leaving the trees behind, we entered Pelion Gap, eventually levelling out onto a plateau and the highest point on the walk. The guidebook says this is one of the Overland Track's best views. Unfortunately we had a lot of mist in ours, but ahead there was Cathedral Mountain and the Du Cane Range, with Mount Pelion East in the east and Mount Doris in the west with Mount Ossa behind it. According to the old sign we saw there, Pelion Gap is '1,113 m'. I don't know if that means it's the highest point on the track at 1,113 m above sea level, or if there was another 1,113 m more to climb to get to that point. It confused me.

As we climbed higher onto the great plateau at the top, the wind began blowing hard and whipped the falling snow up into a blizzard, which hit us right in the face. All I could see, as we fought our way along, step by step, was a lot of bright white framed by two looming black mountains. The feeling of being at the mercy of nature and its whims was almost overwhelming. For that brief climb I realised that not only was it possible for me to die here – for us *all* to die here – but that someday I *would* die, and I don't mean the simple knowledge that 'everyone dies eventually'; it was a deeper awakening to my own mortality – that I cannot escape it. For the first time I really thought about the possible consequences of nobody knowing where we are, and that we aren't supposed to be here. What if the track gets closed in the middle of winter because of some safety issue? What was Alice thinking, getting us into this? Did she really think she could take on the cruel power of the elements and be certain of winning? What are we doing here?

But I carried on – there was nothing else for it – slow and steady, wearing my sunglasses against the wind, concentrating on moving forwards and getting through this possibly dangerous patch of weather, like walking on a narrow footpath next to a busy roadway: get through the task as quickly but as carefully as possible and it would be done, hopefully never to be repeated. On, on, on.

Just before we started the descent into the valley on the other side, we stopped to take some photos of each other. Pelion Gap is also about the halfway point of the Overland Track, and Yvonne announced that she felt a real sense of achievement at having come so far. I was just glad to be through the worst of the gap, but it *was* a big milestone we'd just ticked off. Strangely, a great sense of loss came with this, and I felt depressed. I remember looking at Yvonne, and then at Mary and Alice, to try to work out what they were feeling. But it was impossible; their faces were too wrapped up for me to see their expressions. I began to wonder if the walk itself was coming to represent my grief over David's death. Perhaps, now it's half over, I only have half of the time I allowed to feel sorry for myself left. I don't normally think like this. I wonder if Alice ever does. Is that why she insisted we come on this trip? I'd find it hard to believe, but who knows what really lurks in people's hearts? And all that.

Once through Pelion Gap, we began descending, going south-east for 1.5 km into Pinestone Valley and across Pinestone Creek. Then it was up a bit and, finally, an easy downward trek for about 2.2 km, heading south-east through more lovely forest until we reached Kia Ora Hut.

Night

It's gotten dark. The only light comes from our head torches and a few tea-light candles Mary thought to bring. I'm finding the atmosphere oppressive, like the silence of the bush is somehow quieter tonight, and the night is … darker? Maybe I'm just feeling a little spooked (Yvonne's been reading to us from *The Book of the Dead* again, which I'll have to borrow later to copy from), but – no, that's no explanation – they're just words, after all. Mind you, we were taken a bit by surprise when Yvonne read:

> O you who cause the perfected souls to draw near to
> the House of Osiris, may you cause the excellent soul
> of David to draw near with you to the House of Osiris.
> May he hear as you hear, may he see as you see, may he
> stand as you stand, may he sit as you sit.

'What do you mean the "soul of David"?' said Alice, interrupting. 'David who?'

'*David* David,' said Yvonne. '*Our* David.' She continued:

> O you who give bread and beer to the perfected souls
> in the House of Osiris, may you give bread and beer at
> all seasons to the soul of David, who is vindicated with
> all the gods of the Thinite nome, and who is vindicated
> with you.
>
> O you who open a path and open up roads for the
> perfected souls in the House of Osiris, open a path for
> him, open up roads for the soul of David in company
> with you. May he come in freely, may he go out in
> peace from the House of Osiris, without being repelled
> or turned back. May he go in favoured, may he come
> out loved, may he be vindicated, may his commands be
> done in the House of Osiris, may he go and speak with
> you, may he be a spirit with you, may no fault be
> found in him, for the balance is voided of his misdoings.

'What's a "finite gnome" when it's at home?' I asked, making Mary giggle nervously.

'Stop it!' cried Alice, who'd sat glumly through the rest of the recitation.

'What?' said Yvonne.

'You don't need to bring David into this nonsense.'

'It's only a bit of fun. They said these spells so the dead would have a good time in the afterlife. I thought I'd say some for David, as a send-off sort of thing. Don't tell me you're superstitious about it.'

'Of course I'm not. I just don't want to talk about David right now.'

'I thought that's why we were here. Why did you make us come on the trip, then?'

'I mean,' said Alice, 'I don't want you being frivolous with his memory. Mixing him in with this nonsense.' She pointed at the book Yvonne held in her hands.

'Ah,' said Yvonne, 'but can you be so sure it's only nonsense? Strange wonders are yours to perform. Or something.' She went on cheerily, flipping through the pages. 'No one really knows if there's some sort of survival after we die. I mean, who knows, maybe spell one twenty-five is just what David needs right now: "What should be said when arriving at this Hall of Justice, purging David of all the evil which he has done, and beholding the faces of the gods".' She continued reading aloud:

> Hail to you, great god, Lord of Justice! I have come to
> you, my lord, that you may bring me so that I may see
> your beauty, for I know you and I know your name,
> and I know the names of the forty-two gods of those
> who are with you in this Hall of Justice, who live on
> those who cherish evil and who gulp down their blood
> on that day of the reckoning of characters in the
> presence of Wennefer.

'What do you mean "evil"?' said Alice. 'What evil do you think David has done?'

'And who's Wennefer?' I said.

'I have no idea,' said Yvonne. 'But I don't think it means real evil, just any misdemeanours. Here, keep listening.'

> Behold the double son of the Songstresses; Lord of
> Truth is your name. Behold, I have come to you, I have
> brought you truth, I have repelled falsehood for you. I

have not done falsehood against men, I have not
impoverished my associates, I have done no wrong in
the Place of Truth, I have not learnt that which is not, I
have done no evil, I have not daily made labour in
excess of what was due to be done for me, my name
has not reached the offices of those who control slaves,
I have not deprived the orphan of his property, I have
not done what the gods detest, I have not calumniated
a servant to his master, I have not caused pain, I have
not made hungry, I have not made to weep, I have not
killed, I have not commanded to kill, I have not …

'Do give it a rest,' said Alice.

'But you get the point,' said Yvonne. 'David hasn't done any of
those things, it's just that the afterlife doesn't know it.'

… I have not made suffering for anyone, I have not
lessened the food-offerings in the temples, I have not
destroyed the loaves of the gods, I have not taken away
the food of the spirits, I have not copulated, I have not
misbehaved …

I am pure, pure, pure, pure! My purity is the purity
of that great phoenix which is in Heracleopolis,
because I am indeed the nose of the Lord of Wind who
made all men live on that day of completing the Sacred
Eye in Heliopolis …

Okay, I'm starting to get a bit sick of copying these things out
now. Why couldn't Yvonne have picked shorter passages to read to
us? I'd edit them down, but it feels as if they're becoming such a part
of our experience on this trip that I've wanted to record them here.

'Oh, do stop it,' said Mary. 'You shouldn't be reading that. You're ... you're being morbid.'

'No I'm not,' said Yvonne. 'This is all positive stuff. And *I* want to talk about David. It's not my fault – or his fault, either – that he's dead. I'd like to think that if he's conscious anywhere at all right now that he's all right. I hope his purity *is* of that great phoenix which is' – she consulted the text – 'in Heracleopolis. Wouldn't you want that, Alice?'

I couldn't tell if she was joking or not.

'Now you've upset Mary as well,' said Alice. 'Just pack it in, Yvonne.'

'Pack what in?' said Yvonne. 'Reading what's in here?' She flung the book on the table. 'Or daring to mention the fact that David's dead? Because neither of you seem to be able to acknowledge it. It did happen – and I, for one, miss him, and wish he was here with us now.'

'Of course we acknowledge what happened, you idiot,' said Alice. She was getting uncharacteristically worked up. 'It's just that ... just ... Ah, I don't have to explain myself to you.'

Yvonne leaned back in her seat, the light from her head torch darting across the ceiling.

'No,' she said, 'that's true. But what if he is? What if he actually is?'

'What do you mean?'

'I mean if David's spirit is following us as we do this walk, he might be with us right now. This very second he might be looking in at us through that window.'

Just as she finished saying this, I thought, *We're all going to look, aren't we?* Even though none of us actually think there'll be anything except blackness behind that pane of glass, still we're all going to look over at it. And we did. Even Yvonne looked, which I thought spoiled the effect if she was trying to shock or frighten us, as I suspected she was. I wish she'd stop baiting Alice.

But what if she wasn't trying to spook us? Did she expect to see something in the window too? If so, what's her thinking? Does she really believe David could be here with us? I wish he was here too, but that's an uncomfortable thought. Mary certainly doesn't like the idea. She's gone into the sleeping area, presumably to get away from us and our unsettling talk. Though, of course, with the hut being so small she can still hear everything we are saying.

Alice just stared at Yvonne. 'Have you completely lost your mind?' she said.

And of course there *was* nothing at the window, except condensation and our own weak blurry reflections. The human preoccupation with death and what comes after it – indeed, wanting there to *be* something to come after – is why we have things like *The Book of the Dead* and countless other options for what to believe. I understand people's need to see their loved ones again, but I don't understand how they can be scared of the idea that they themselves mightn't go anywhere after death. If there's nothing, then there's nothing to worry about. I think I read somewhere that the Buddhists believe obliteration – if that's the right word – is the ultimate goal of existence. After all, people don't worry about being asleep, and that's a state of nothingness, as far as our consciousness is concerned. It's just a dreamless sleep.

Alice has told me she agrees with me about the fear of nothingness, but I don't know if that's merely in principle or she really doesn't think there could be an afterlife. Is that why she got annoyed with Yvonne? Because that means there can't be ghosts, either. At least – so I wonder – not ghosts that are a non-physical survival of dead human beings – or dogs, or cats, horses, monkeys, rats ... And if ghosts are real *ghost* ghosts, then what's the point in

them if you can't talk to them properly? I don't see the use in bumping into them for a few seconds in a darkened house if you can't ask them things.

Yvonne ignored her, and began to recite again.

'Spell number ninety-two, "for opening the tomb to David's soul and shade so that he may go out into the day and have power in his legs".'

Sounds useful.

> Open and close! O you who sleep, open and close for
> my soul according to the command of Horus. O Eye
> of Horus, save me, establish my beauty on the vertex of
> Re. O Far-strider whose legs extend, make a way for
> me here, for my flesh is made ready.

Later

Something disturbing has just happened. Mary was looking through the photos we've taken so far, particularly the ones we took today, and came back into the cooking area clutching her camera.

'Look,' she said. 'Look at this, quick. These pictures we took after the walk through the blizzard ... See ... ? And this one. Do you see it? Go back to the first one again.'

At first we didn't understand what she was talking about. Then Yvonne noticed something.

'Oh! Is that ... ? Flip through the others again. Yes.'

'What?!' said Alice.

'That,' said Mary, pointing.

In a shot of Alice, Mary and myself – and then a few seconds later in another two of Alice, Mary and Yvonne – there was a black/brown smudge of an object in the distance behind us. It was shaped like a human being. The pictures were taken from slightly different angles, including a failed selfie shot of all of us – but the figure wasn't in that last one – so it was difficult to judge if it was moving or not.

'Do you think it's a person?' said Yvonne.

Alice took the camera and looked more closely at the images. She stood staring at them for what seemed quite a long time. Then she looked over at the window. Yvonne immediately turned her head torch off and Mary copied her.

'The thing is, though,' said Alice at last, 'if that is someone, what is he or she doing now? If they're walking the track, they ought to have arrived here ages ago.'

'Maybe they're doing the same thing as us,' said Mary, 'staying clear of the huts because they know they're not supposed to be here.'

'I'm more worried about it being a ranger.'

'If it was a ranger they'd definitely use the huts, wouldn't they?' said Yvonne. 'That's what that locked door is outside; it's the rangers' quarters next door.'

'Hopefully they are doing maintenance on the track,' said Alice, 'so they will want to stay close to where they're working. Or they might have turned onto a side trail somewhere. There might be another rangers' hut.'

Then something occurred to me.

'What if it's just a normal walker and they saw *us* here,' I said, 'so they went to camp somewhere else? They might think *we're* rangers, or something.'

'Or even saw us on the track earlier,' said Yvonne. 'He could have come from one of the side trails that link up with Pelion Hut? If it *is* a he. Maybe the side trails aren't closed like the main track.'

'What if something has happened to him in the snow?' said Mary.

Again Alice sat silently. She seemed to be thinking. Then she went into the bunk area and started pulling her coat down from where she'd hung it on a rafter.

'What are you doing?' said Mary.

'I don't think there is anything to be worried about,' said Alice. 'If it is a ranger and they find us, we will simply play dumb about the track being closed. But I think I will have a look around to see if anyone has been about. It will be as well to know if anyone is coming up behind us.'

'I'll come with you,' said Yvonne.

'No, no, I'll be quieter on my own. I won't be long; don't worry. I'll just have a little look around.'

She finished dressing, pulled her boots on, and stepped outside clutching a torch. We watched from the doorway as she disappeared into the dark. Then we closed the hut door and waited.

And we're still waiting. I'm writing this to keep myself busy while we do. Mary is sat on the floor by the door and Yvonne is pacing about the room. She had been sat next to me, again flipping through *The Book of the Dead*, and had started to read out another section, but stopped after a while without Mary having to say anything. I'll copy out the 'spell' in full, inserting David's name as Yvonne did – number twenty-seven, 'Spell for not permitting a man's heart to be taken from him in the realm of the dead':

O you who take away hearts and accuse hearts, who
recreate a man's heart (in respect of) what he has done,
he is forgetful of himself through what you have done.
Hail to you, lords of eternity, founders of everlasting!
Do not take David's heart with your fingers wherever
his heart may be. You shall not raise any matter harmful
to him, because as for this heart of David's, this heart

belongs to one whose names are great, whose words
are mighty, who possesses his members. He sends out
his heart which controls his body, his heart is
announced to the gods, for David's heart is his own, he
has power over it, and he will not say what he has
done. He himself has power over his members, his
heart obeys him, for he is your lord and you are in his
body, you shall not turn aside. I command you to obey
me in the realm of the dead, even I, David, who am
vindicated in peace and vindicated in the beautiful
West in the domain of eternity.

The beam of my head torch is the only light showing now. Mary
blew the candles out. I'd have thought she would have wanted to
keep them lit. It'll make it more difficult for Alice to find her way
back, but neither Yvonne nor I said anything about it. I can't explain
why I didn't object, other than the fact that we should probably be
conserving them. Somehow it seemed like something I might have
done myself, so I found I didn't have the moral authority. And they
are her candles.

A Little Later

Alice is back and I'm in bed. The atmosphere brightened the
moment we saw it was her, covered with a dusting of snow.

'Well, that wasn't as cold as I thought it was going to be,' she said.
'It was all the gear I had on, I suppose.

'So. I had a wander around the hut area and checked the tent
platforms and the helipad. I even went backwards and forwards over
the main track for a bit. But I could only see the tracks we would
have made ourselves, though the new snow is starting to cover things.

There were no lights. Not that I thought there would be. Why is it so dark in here?'

Yvonne relit the candles while Alice finished getting out of her wet-weather things.

'What do we do now?' said Mary.

'Nothing,' said Alice. 'I don't see that there is anything *to* be done. Maybe there was someone on the track, maybe there wasn't. We will just get up extra early in the morning and be on our way.'

It does seem the only thing to do. My only worry is that someone might arrive in the middle of the night while we're asleep. The huts don't lock, so I leant some packs up against the door, with a few clangy metal things balanced on top, so if anyone does come in we'll be woken up. Hopefully. But I can't see that anyone will come now. No one will want to be walking in the dark and the snow. They'll have camped somewhere. I made myself walk over to the composting toilets – rather than just going somewhere close to the hut – to prove to myself that I could go out alone. And, of course, that smudge on the photo might not be anyone at all.

Time to switch out my light and try to go to sleep. The others have all gone quiet while I've been writing this, but I have a feeling it'll take us a long time to relax enough to nod off.

DAY FIVE

Late Morning

Yvonne has gone missing! We don't know what to do.

When we woke this morning we found the packs moved away from the door and the metal things neatly stacked on a table. Yvonne's sleeping bag was empty. Alice was up first and thought she'd only gone out to the toilet or to fetch water but, when she hadn't come back after fifteen minutes, Alice went out to find her. When she couldn't, she came back to get Mary and me and we searched the area as best we could. But the ground was completely blanketed with snow and, with the exception of Alice's own set of tracks going once around the hut and to the toilets and back, we could find no trace of anything. It appears she's been gone for some time.

We returned to the hut and looked through her things for anything that might tell us where she'd gone, but there was nothing.

All her stuff is still here, including her phone, so there's no point in trying that, with or without a signal. We even found her jacket and boots, which especially perplexes and worries us, although we aren't completely sure what she brought with her in the way of clothing.

She's definitely not inside the hut – there's nowhere to hide. Nor are there any signs she's been 'taken away', which is a possibility we've considered. It was the first thing Mary said when Alice told us what had happened. Could it have something to do with the figure in the photos? I've had another look at them and I still can't make up my mind if it's actually a person or just a rock or something. No one heard anything from my intruder alarm during the night, and it seems absurd that someone would kidnap a woman on the Overland Track while her three friends were in the same hut. Where could they take her? How could they avoid leaving tracks in the snow? You'd think she'd have a hundred opportunities to raise the alarm. It's impossible. But it has to be more likely than the alternative: that she's continued on by herself without telling any of us. Mind you, things did get a little tense between her and Alice last night. But that's no reason to go off without saying anything.

So at the moment we don't know what to do. We're trying to prepare and eat some breakfast, but I don't feel hungry. There's no one else here to help us, and calling someone outside of the park means we'll be found out for being here in the first place. That's if we were *able* to call outside the park. I climbed the steps to the toilets with all our phones earlier (Mary didn't bring one), but none of them could get a signal. I hope Alice is happy with herself. She might be used to taking such big risks, but I'm not. The only resource we have left is her personal locator thing. But then, what if Yvonne does come back? We'll have caused a lot of fuss and given the game away for nothing. You're only supposed to use those things in a real emergency. Can we really say that this is what that is yet? It seems so impossible that Yvonne can have really gone missing that surely she must turn up again, and then everything will be all right. But it's such a gamble, and I don't know where to put my money. Why on earth did I agree to come along on this trip? Because it's what David wanted us to do? What sort of reasoning is that?

And even if we did know that Yvonne had set off on the track again, we can't be certain which direction she's gone in – forwards or backwards. We'll have to split up to search both ways. I'm inclined to think she hasn't done this, but that means she could be anywhere in the bush by now.

Alice just said she wants us to go out searching again after we've eaten. She's worried about Yvonne not having her coat or boots with her. At least she's worried about *something*. She's studying the map right now.

Mary didn't seem to want to go out again, which I find surprising given the circumstances, but as soon as I started talking about her staying behind by herself in case Yvonne comes back, she suddenly wanted to come with us.

Later

We're back from the second search, but there's absolutely no sign of Yvonne. The hut is sat in one of several small clearings, the others being for the nearby tent platforms and toilet block, all of which are surrounded with light scrub. It's a very claustrophobic, closed-in space, and sound doesn't travel very well. The thick snow has turned the landscape into a completely colourless black and white. The contrast is so strong that it fairly burns into your vision with its intensity. But we have searched it all again and again, been everywhere that we can think of that she might have gone to explore, and have found nothing. Alice even went down to the nearby creek

in case she went there. So unless she has deliberately wandered off into the bush and gotten lost … But, even then, surely she would have had the sense to stay put and call for us, or to wait until she heard us calling her. But why on earth *should* she leave the camp area without any of us? It would be so easy to lose your way out there in the snow, and none of us knows what the terrain is like. It doesn't make any sense. This time we even shone a torch down the chutes of the composting toilets!

Alice and Mary aren't talking to each other, and I don't feel like speaking to either of them right now – I've gotten sick of having to listen to them fight. Mary was bitching how stupid it was of Alice to get us to sneak onto the track when she knew there'd be no one here to help us in an emergency. And if Mary hadn't said it, I probably would have. True, recriminations aren't going to help anyone right now – certainly not Yvonne – but something *has* gone wrong and Alice doesn't seem to know what to do. Alice! – who *always* knows what to do.

But, of course, Alice didn't force us to come; we all knew the dangers of walking here when we weren't supposed to. Alice didn't hide anything from us, but she was so insistent we do it right away and it felt so important to her – so important to David – that we all agreed to go. Now it appears sentiment might have been our undoing. It's true she's never let us down before, but that doesn't really mean much out here, alone in the snow-covered wild. Why *is* this trip so important to her? Why did it have to be done right now? She's never said, and I don't have the force of will to ask her. And why would Yvonne go off on her own – if that's what she's done? Questions – I only have questions.

Later Still

Alice has gone out to search yet again. She said she didn't want Mary and me to leave the hut this time in case Yvonne comes back, but I know she just doesn't want us with her. We didn't object, and it feels better knowing someone is out there looking, even though it seems impossible it'll do any good. Or perhaps I should say it alleviates our guilt at not being out there looking every moment there is. I don't mind being out there in the wet and the snow and the mud – it's not knowing where we should be looking that depresses me. If she'd taken her things and there was some indication as to which way she'd gone, we'd be out there now trying to catch up with her. Mind you, if she'd taken her things with her, we probably wouldn't be so concerned – just pissed off that she'd gone off on her own. It's the strangeness of it that worries me; it's an impossible thing that's happened. It makes me think she might suddenly appear back in her sleeping bag as if nothing had happened.

With Alice gone I'm glad I'm not alone here, but I'm worried about Mary. She's very jumpy and I know that sort of thing can be contagious. I'm doing a good enough job of creeping myself out; I certainly don't need any more help.

I've been reading back over the last few pages of this diary and I don't want it to sound like I don't understand how serious our situation is. I do realise – and I only want to have to say this once – that Yvonne might be dead right now, and may have been dead for some time. But even that doesn't properly explain things. It only explains why she hasn't come back. I'm trying hard not to let that thought take root in my mind until we absolutely know it to be true – and, even then, not until we're off the track. I'm glad I have this diary to keep myself occupied. I need to find something for Mary to do as well.

Evening

Alice didn't come back until it was almost dark. She looked very tired.

There was no sign of Yvonne – not that I thought there would be.

'There is nothing we can do now it's dark,' she said. Her face was invisible in the gloom of the hut – Mary and I hadn't bothered to turn on our lights or light the candles. 'So we will stay here again tonight. If she doesn't turn up by morning we will have to walk out and get help to search for her.'

I thought it was too urgent for that.

'I think we should activate your emergency beacon,' I said.

Alice looked taken aback. 'We don't need to do that!'

'She's been missing *all day*,' I said. 'And she wouldn't go off like that. She wouldn't go anywhere without the rest of us – certainly not without her things.'

'We'll get back on the track tomorrow and, if we don't find her, we will ... well, we'll cross that ... But she's gone on ahead of us. She must have gone on ahead.'

If she has, it'll be because of Alice being such a bitch to her last night.

'I can't believe you can think that,' I said. 'She must be stuck somewhere. She probably needs help *now*, if it isn't already ... I don't think we'll find her tomorrow.'

'What do *you* think?' Alice said to Mary.

'I didn't know you had an emergency beacon,' said Mary. 'Yes, turn it on! I don't care if we aren't supposed to be here; they can only fine us.'

We both looked at Alice expectantly.

Alice sighed. 'Well, we can't.'

'What do you mean?' I said.

'I can't turn it on because I didn't get one.'

There was silence.

'But ... but you said you already had one,' I said.

'I said I was going to *buy* one. But when I went to, they were so hideously expensive, and I didn't ... I didn't think we'd really need one. There were going to be four of us doing the walk, so I thought the others could look after anyone who hurt themselves. I've ... I've never had a problem before. I'm sorry; I thought we would be all right.'

'Oh, no,' said Mary. 'What are we going to do now?'

I was furious with Alice just then. Why couldn't she have told us? If she wasn't going to buy one, then maybe we could've made other arrangements. She's always speaking for everyone else, always deciding what is best for everyone. Well, this time it looks like she might have killed poor Yvonne.

But there was no point in arguing about it. The thing was done, and it would only be wasting time. I could think of only one other option open to us now.

'I'm going to break into the rangers' room,' I said. 'There must be a radio in there we can use.'

I started to walk towards the door and Alice sprinted after me.

'It's locked,' she said. 'I checked it when I was looking for Yvonne.'

'I know,' I said, opening the door of the hut and stepping out onto the verandah. 'That's why we'll have to break in.'

'You can't kick the door in.'

'We've got no choice now. It's an emergency.'

I backed up in the little space there was and rammed my shoulder into the door like they do in the movies, but it was completely solid – and I hurt my shoulder.

'See,' said Alice. 'It's not going to work.'

I tried again, ramming it even harder.

'Oh, do stop!' she cried. 'You're not going to be able to do it.'

'We've got to try something,' I said. 'Yvonne *must* be in trouble if she's been missing for this long. It doesn't matter if we get caught now; we need to get people searching for her.'

'Well, yes …' Alice began.

But I wasn't listening. I stepped off the verandah into the dark, switching on my head torch.

'Where are you going?'

'I'm looking for something,' I said.

I shone my light under the hut (we'd looked for Yvonne under there as well), but had to go right around to the other side before I found what I was looking for: a good-sized rock. Returning with it, I decided there was nothing else left to do but smash the door in. At least, I was going to try to do *something* with it. I'd also taken a look at the window of the rangers' room, but it was covered over with metal grilling.

'Move out of the way,' I said.

'What is that going to do?' said Alice.

'I don't know.'

'Wouldn't the rangers carry their radios around with them?' Mary appeared in the hut doorway. 'In case they get into trouble when they're on the track.'

'There's got to be one in there,' I said, and began bashing at the lock with my rock a few times, but it was obviously pointless.

'See,' said Alice. 'You are just making a mess. Now, come back inside. We have got to keep our heads in all this.'

I sighed, defeated. But it was more that I felt thwarted by Alice's attitude. Why isn't she as concerned about Yvonne as she appears to be with us being caught by the rangers?

As walking out to find help now appears to be our only remaining option, I'll have another go at breaking into the rangers' room when we get to the next hut – unless I think of a way to get into the one here during the night.

Anyway, I gave in and now we're eating dinner. I'm having more of those scrambled eggs with instant mashed potato. The potato has the consistency of soap powder, but I'm hungrier than I thought I'd be.

Later Again

We're all going to bed now, as none of us feels much like talking. Also, I want us to be on our way as soon as it gets light.

I simply can't understand what could have happened to Yvonne. There's nowhere to go except along the track. But why would she do that without telling anyone? And there just *isn't* anyone else here for her to go off with. It's crazy. That black/brown thing in the photo must have been a bush or a rock or something. It must have.

Early Morning

Something else has just happened. There was someone outside the hut – we all heard it. Mary woke me up in the dark, putting her hand over my mouth when I began making a noise.

'Shh,' she said. 'Listen – outside.'

When at last I realised where I was, I listened. But there was nothing.

I heard Alice stir, slowly unzipping her sleeping bag.

Then there it was. Alice stopped still – we all did – and I really did feel the hairs on my neck tingle and bristle. It was the clear and unmistakable sound of footsteps on the verandah outside. Step – step

– step. They began to slowly walk back and forth, as if whoever it was was investigating the hut, but didn't attempt to come inside.

My first thought was that it was Yvonne. But there was something about the way it moved. Step – step – step: each was as definite and full of purpose as the last, each like the links in a chain. If it was Yvonne, what was she doing, why didn't she come inside?

Alice quickly slipped from her sleeping bag, grabbed her torches, and began creeping towards the door. Apparently she also thought the behaviour was a little too odd to be Yvonne. I slid into a sitting position as Alice paused for a few moments, presumably waiting for the footsteps to sound again. Part of me wanted to be over there with her, backing her up against whoever was outside, yet I was afraid to make the slightest noise.

Then Alice quickly switched on her head torch and the one she held in her hand and opened the door, springing out with a great primal sort of roaring noise. I quickly wriggled out of my own sleeping bag and felt for my torch. I heard Mary move, but I couldn't see what she was doing.

When I reached Alice she was standing in the doorway scanning the snow-covered bush with her lights. I looked as well, not knowing what to expect. It was continuing to snow quite hard, but nothing else was moving. It was all completely silent. After a few moments it became clear there was no one out there – there was nothing there at all.

We cautiously stepped to the edge of the verandah and shone our torches further out over the landscape. There were no footprints that I could see, although the ground was quite lumpy. I wondered if I'd somehow imagined the sound of footsteps, or been mistaken about what the sound had been. But Alice and Mary had heard something too, and it really did sound just like someone was moving about out there. I followed Alice as she went around the hut looking for anything out of place. Not so much as a possum was stirring.

'What's going on?' I whispered.

Alice merely grunted and she wouldn't look at me. I suppose there was nothing she *could* say.

We arrived back at the verandah and found Mary nervously peering from a crack in the doorway. She had closed it as much as her head would allow.

'Where did you go?' she whispered. 'What's happening?'

'Don't know,' I said. 'We didn't see anything.'

'Aah,' she groaned, and her body seemed to deflate into itself. 'What's happening to us here?'

'It sounded like footsteps to you, didn't it?' I said. 'It did to me, but maybe it was an animal.'

Alice was scanning the trees with her torches again.

'Anyway,' I said, 'it's gone now, so … I'm going back to bed. It's freezing.'

I wasn't comfortable being out there any longer, and there was no point in upsetting Mary – she was already creeped out – though I knew I wouldn't be able to sleep. And it *was* very cold.

Alice lingered a little longer, and then she too came back in and closed the door.

We all drifted back to our bunks but no one got into their sleeping bag.

'Was it – was it Yvonne, do you think? Out there?' said Mary.

'Couldn't have been,' said Alice. 'She would have come inside.'

'What if she wasn't sure it was us, though? What if she's worried about running into a ranger, or whatever?'

'Oh,' I said. I hadn't thought of that. 'Maybe we should have called out her name?' But I knew I wouldn't have been able to do that. Not in that atmosphere.

'There weren't any footprints in the snow,' said Alice, a little petulantly I thought. 'It must have just been an animal coming down from the roof, or something like that.'

Mary and I looked up at the ceiling. The light from our head torches danced over the wooden beams.

'What sort of animal makes a sound like that?' said Mary. But neither Alice nor I could give her an answer.

We didn't say very much to each other for the next little while. I suppose we didn't know what to do with ourselves, and the footsteps had really weirded us out. Could someone be following us after all? But how could they not have left footprints in the snow?

Then suddenly we heard them again, clear and deliberate on the verandah. It was so much worse the second time because, knowing now that there were no tracks, I knew they were an impossible thing. They could not *be*. My blood ran cold – nor has it warmed up still! Mary gasped, and I might even have done the same thing, but Alice slid over to the door once more, flung it open and sprang out, shining her torches. She gave another inarticulate cry, this time as if she was trying to batter anyone out there with the power of her voice, and called, 'Who's there?!'

There was no reply. Just the ever-present – and now eerily so – cold indifferent silence of the falling snow. Alice stood shining her torches about and breathing hard.

I noticed Mary was now getting very upset – I don't blame her! – then, when Alice called out again, 'Yvonne, are you there?!' she jumped up like a startled sparrow.

'Don't!' she hissed, darting across the floor towards Alice, then stopping and taking a few steps back again. 'Don't call out.'

I don't think Alice was paying much attention then, so I went over to Mary.

'Why not?' I said. 'What do you think it is?'

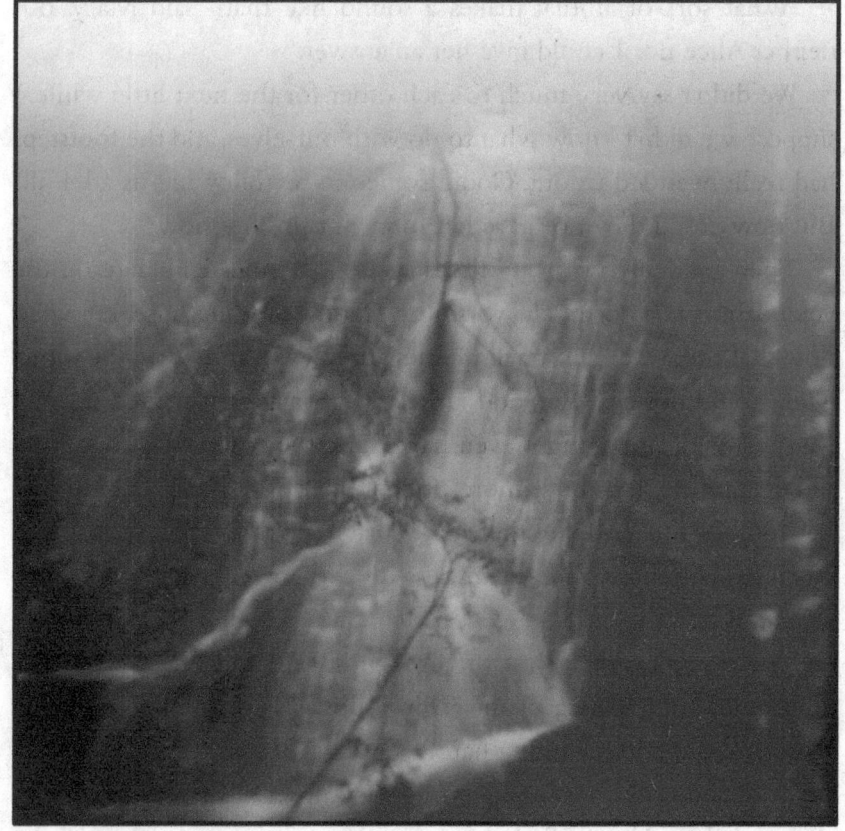

She shivered. 'What did she have to bring that book with her for? She shouldn't have read out that stuff about David. Not out loud.'

'What?'

My mind started to boggle with all sorts of sinister possibilities as to what might be out there in the forest and the snow. For a while now I've been trying to rid myself of the idea that Yvonne's disappearing – especially now we've heard these uncanny footsteps – might have something supernatural about it. I've tried to remain rational, tried to stop myself dwelling on anything that could make me more fearful, but Mary's behaviour – and even Alice's, to some extent – is really messing with my mind. Nor have I been able to come up with another explanation for what's happening. It doesn't make sense: we've heard footsteps but there are no marks in the snow; Yvonne has vanished but where could she have gone to? And I keep thinking of that black/brown figure in the background of the Pelion Gap photos. I'm beginning to question whether I can trust my senses anymore.

Alice came back inside and shut the door.

'Pull yourself together, Mary,' she said. 'I don't know what is going on – it's very strange, true – but we shouldn't be afraid of it. We just need to keep a cool head. Tomorrow we will get back on the track and report Yvonne missing when we get to the end.'

It's comforting to know at least one of us isn't going to pieces, and it's quietened Mary down. Still, it would be good to keep an eye on what's going on inside Mary's head. I hope she won't mind me saying, but she needs a lot of reassurance when she's out of her comfort zone, and I think Alice's personality can overwhelm her, so she keeps a lot bottled up. She responds well to Alice, though; in fact, with the two of them being such close friends, I'm feeling a bit isolated, in an emotional sense. It feels lonely enough out here. I don't know, maybe I'm overreacting, but I worry that if I'm to ever get out of here it will need to be done through my own resilience.

Day Six

Morning

Nothing else happened after that – no more footsteps. We barricaded the door with our packs, and I even managed to get some sleep just as the dawn was beginning to creep up. When it came time to leave my sleeping bag I found it quite difficult. What a difference the light of day can make: even isolated out here, with the panic of last night still fresh in my mind, things felt a lot better.

We have decided to leave Yvonne's pack here in the hut, along with a note in case she does happen to come back, or someone else finds it. I'm finding this a bit upsetting; it's as if we're leaving her behind, or that we don't have any confidence in finding her again. But we can't bring it with us; it's difficult enough carrying the 16 kg of weight we each have already. I'll have to carry our tent by myself now as well – no taking it in turns. It will mean leaving Yvonne without one – if she returns – but the rest of us can't possibly fit into one tent.

JAMES MCLACHLAN

Midday – Du Cane Hut

We are now at Du Cane Hut. *Du Cane?* It's an old trappers' hut made
from timber shingles in a clearing surrounded by a forest of myrtle
and leatherwood trees. It has an enormous fireplace, which tells you
just how cold it must get out here sometimes, and there's a lot of
graffiti on the woodwork inside. Some of it goes back to the
seventies. I ran my bare hand over it, feeling its age and shrivelled
dryness. Beside the look of it, it just feels as though an enormous
amount of people have passed the night within its walls. Now it's
only slept in in emergencies, and it feels like it would be very
draughty, especially at night. It has a bit of an odd abandoned feeling
about it as well, as if it's too old and doesn't belong to the present. I
feel like I can never 'know' it like the other huts. It's like it's one of
the features of the walk, rather than one of the facilities for doing it.
Of course, it *is* a feature, but this one is man-made, so it feels
different.

Leaving Kia Ora Hut (come to think of it, what sort of a name is
Kia Ora as well?) was a big relief, but it was also distressing because
it's the only place where Yvonne knows to look for us. But we
couldn't sit around indefinitely; we have to get help to conduct a
more thorough search than we've been able to do so far.

Not far from the hut we crossed a bridge over Kia Ora Creek,
turned to the south-east and walked for 2 km. Most of the way was
through thick dark forest, with only occasional patches of snow
where it had been able to fall through the canopy. Then we broke
into a misty clearing blanketed with snow, with Du Cane Hut at the
far end, obscured by some small trees. I presume this is a spot where
people stop off to take photos, etc., but we're still too near to Kia Ora
Hut for my liking. I think we're lingering in case we find any sign of
Yvonne, so I'm feeling torn between going and staying a bit longer.

JAMES MCLACHLAN

Afternoon – near Bert Nichols Hut

From Du Cane Hut we went eastwards, turning to the south-east and entering a thick forest of myrtle trees. After about 1.6 km we came to a junction leading down to the D'Alton and Fergusson waterfalls, but of course we didn't have time to go look at them. After another 700 m there was another junction, this time leading down to the Hartnett Falls. Again, we didn't go to look. The track continued west, gently climbing for 1.4 km through forest, and crossed Campfire Creek. A further climb – 800 m or so – brought us to the south side of Du Cane Gap and, once out of there, the track descended steeply for 1.8 km through another myrtle forest until we reached Bert Nichols Hut.

For a while we debated if we should stay inside it or not. I thought it was a good idea because we'd have a better chance of meeting anyone who might turn up and could help us, but Alice is apparently still worried that we aren't supposed to be on the track, and is making us stay in the tents. I'd have thought we were all well past that by this stage, but Mary doesn't want to sleep in the hut either – which I'm not as shocked about – so that's what we're doing, only she was more blunt about her feelings.

'We can't stay in there,' she said. 'It'll know where we are.'

I'd caught her looking back over the track many times today, and I knew it was more to make sure we weren't being followed by anyone than it was to look for signs of Yvonne. I found *myself* doing it. In fact, if I'm honest, I'd rather not stay in the hut either, but I don't want the others to think I'm willing to give up on rescuing Yvonne simply because I'm frightened. Whatever it was that came to the hut last night can't have meant us any good, but then – oh, I don't know – was it our imaginations or not? Can there be a rational explanation for what's been happening? I can't make up my mind.

Before we put the tents up, we went over to the hut to see if we could find a radio. I insisted on that at least, and the others weren't in a position to say no.

Bert Nichols Hut – formerly Windy Ridge Hut, or built on the site of Windy Ridge Hut, I'm not sure which – turned out to be huge, though surprisingly it only has room to sleep twenty-four people. It has a drying room where you hang up your wet things, and a huge dining room with a sculpture of leaves on the ceiling. Alice said after spending a week on the track looking at nothing but fucking leaves they could've chosen something else. Also the bunks in the bedrooms are painted a shiny black. This isn't important, but I found it striking, as none of the other huts have bunks like that.

With the greater size of this hut I'm sure it would have been even more unnerving and spooky to be spending the night there – just the three of us – so I'm especially glad we're not doing it now.

We found the rangers' room, but it was locked up even more securely than at Kia Ora. It really seems the only way we're going to find any help is by finishing the walk. This isn't fun anymore. I could never have imagined anything like this happening when we started out on this trip.

We've found a hidden-away spot to pitch the tents, near a spring so we won't have to go to the tanks at the hut to get water. I'm the only one in our tent now that Yvonne has gone, and the reason for her absence has increased my sense of isolation. Plus I'm now solely responsible for setting up and dismantling the thing, and in the snow, too. The routine of pack up, walk, set up, eat, sleep, pack up again, is already getting very tiresome. We're just trying to get to the end now.

Night

I can't believe this is happening to us – now Mary has gone! Alice and I have searched, but she disappeared in the bush in the dark. I really am frightened now – I don't understand what's happening to us. I know Alice is feeling the same, even though she doesn't want to admit it. There are now so many things we don't have an explanation for. It's like I'm in a terrible dream.

I had just been about to fall asleep when I again heard the sound of footsteps, this time crunching over the snow. They slowed and then stopped right in front of our tents, as if whoever it was was curious about them, just like at Kia Ora Hut. Again I wondered if it could be Yvonne come looking for us. But, if so, why doesn't she say anything? I desperately wanted to go out and see what it was, but I was afraid I wouldn't find anything there if I did. I don't think I'd have been able to stand that happening again.

I heard the sound of the tent zipper being opened and I almost screamed with the horror of it, but the sound caught in my throat. Then I realised it was coming from the other tent and I heard someone getting out. There was a flash of light through the wall of my own tent and Alice called, 'Who's there?! Hello?'

Good old Alice.

I quickly got out of my sleeping bag and unzipped my door flap to join her. Mary was getting out of their tent by this time as well.

'Hello?' Alice called again into the bush.

Everything was black except for what was caught in the beam of her head torch. Mary and I switched ours on, revealing a silent world of tightly packed scrub. Someone could have been standing only a few feet away and we might not have seen them.

Alice turned and said, 'You know, this is getting quite tiresome,' though her speech faltered a little.

Then Mary cried out, 'He's never going to go away! He's going to keep following us wherever we go, and he won't stop until he gets all of us. I know it.'

'Who is?' I demanded. 'Who's following us?'

'It's David,' she whispered, and she took a few steps past Alice and me towards the bush. 'He's going to take us all away with him, just like he took Yvonne.'

'Of course it's not David,' said Alice.

'But David's dead,' I said.

I don't know why I said it so bluntly like that. I don't know why I felt it necessary to say it aloud at all. Talk like this was only adding to my already heightened sense of fear, especially with Mary now starting to crack up. Strangely, she herself didn't seem to be scared anymore. The fright she'd felt at the mystery of Yvonne's disappearance and the alarm of the footsteps seemed to have been replaced by something else. I really can't explain this – there was just something about her manner that was different now. Perhaps it was simply the beginnings of her going mad – or the beginnings of me going the same way.

She and Alice looked at me.

'Well, it's true,' I said. 'He is.'

'I know,' said Mary. 'And he's out there watching us, following us whenever we move. Probably Yvonne allowed him to come back with those Egyptian spells of hers.'

'Rubbish,' said Alice.

'But why would he take her?' I said. 'Even if that were true?'

'Who knows what those old words might do?' said Mary. 'He was bound to have felt angry at having died prematurely on that mountain. What if he's angry with *us*?'

'Why would he be – ?' But Alice cut me off.

'Mary,' she said, going over to her, 'shut up. You are becoming hysterical.'

Mary didn't seem to notice her. 'Go away,' she called into the bush. 'I haven't done anything. Alice is the one you want, not me. Take Alice, she's right here!' She started walking into the trees as she called out. 'Alice is the one you want – *she* hurt you. She's right here. Leave Jane and me alone; you've already got Yvonne!'

Alice and I followed, trying to keep up with her, but a few feet into the trees we started to get snagged on branches and bushes, and we soon became separated. The bush was full of flashes of light, the sound of the bending and breaking of branches, and our calls to Mary to come back. No one gave a damn about who might see us now.

After what felt like a couple of minutes I managed to catch up with someone, but it turned out to only be Alice.

'Where is she?' I said.

We stopped moving and the bush was silent once more. Nor could we see any light that wasn't being made by our own torches. I switched mine off and Alice covered hers with her hand. Then she called again, but there was no reply – no sound at all.

'Oh, you've got to be kidding,' I said, and I tried calling her myself. But there was still no answer. 'What do we do now?'

'Keep looking of course,' said Alice. 'She may have knocked herself unconscious on a tree branch or something.'

I turned my light back on and we started moving forwards, scanning the snowy, muddy forest floor, this time keeping close to each other. But after a few minutes it seemed pointless – she could have gone in any direction and we had no way of telling which bits of ground we'd already been over. There were so many lumps and bumps and tree roots that could have been a person fallen down. I didn't even know which way it was back to the tents.

'This is hopeless,' I said. 'We don't know where we are, and I'm freezing.' Neither of us was wearing a coat, and I only had socks on my feet. 'What if — what if she doesn't want to be found?' After all, she *had* been running away from us.

Alice paused for a moment. 'Why wouldn't she want to be found? For what reason?'

She had me there. But then what reason did *Yvonne* have for hiding from us either? If she *was* hiding. We now have two people to report missing when we get out of here, but in my heart — well — I find it difficult to believe they'll be found. I don't see how they could *both* have disappeared like that, not without something having happening to them, so how can I expect them to come back? Perhaps I'm just feeling hopeless at the moment.

We didn't search for much longer. We tried looking for tracks, but in the thicker parts of the forest there wasn't much snow to hold them. Nor do either of us know anything about what you're supposed to look for in a track — except for anything that's clearly a footprint.

Possibly Mary will find her own way back to the tents by the time it gets light. As for Alice and me, we only managed to get back because we stumbled onto Bert Nichols Hut, and could remember our way back to the tents from there. Everything was as we had left it. But no Mary.

I've brought my sleeping bag into Alice's tent (we're sharing now), where I've been writing this. I can't help dwelling on the thought that one of us might be going to disappear too, and most frightening of all is the realisation that the other one will then be left on their own, before she too — possibly — is taken. How will we cope on our own, knowing what might be about to happen to us? And at the same time *not* knowing what might be about to happen to us. We don't know what's become of Yvonne and Mary – I'm frightened to even think about it.

Alice hasn't said anything about Mary's *Alice is the one you want – she hurt you* speech, even though I'm obviously very curious about it. For the moment, I think it best not to say anything. What she said might even be meaningless, just the ravings of someone driven mad by unbearable fear.

DAY SEVEN

Morning

Alice and I have just searched the bush where we last remember seeing Mary, but there's no sign of her. Is this what happened to Yvonne: she just walked out into the forest? It's a natural thing to wonder.

Alice has gone to leave Mary's pack and another note over at Bert Nichols Hut while I cook breakfast. I don't know what she thinks has happened to Yvonne and Mary, but I can tell she didn't really think we'd find Mary today. If she did she would still be out there looking for her, I'm sure of it. She won't talk to me about what's happening to us; she just wants to get out of here, and I think that's what she's wanted to do all morning, despite searching again. Not that I can blame her for that; I do too. But at least we are able to leave one of the tents behind this time, just in case. We're going to be on our way straight after breakfast.

I woke late this morning, which wasn't surprising. Alice was already awake, just lying in her sleeping bag.

'We're supposed to be meeting Liz at the visitor centre this afternoon,' she said. 'We aren't going to make it. I wonder what she will do when we don't show up.'

'Wait until tomorrow, I suppose,' I said. 'We did say we might not make it on time if the weather was playing up. She'll be annoyed, though.'

Alice was quiet for a time, as if she was thinking. 'I'm sorry I brought you and the others into this,' she said at last.

'Why were you so insistent that we do the walk in the first place?' I said.

'That's been preying on my mind all night. I think I wanted us to go somewhere together so I wouldn't have to be alone with my thoughts. I wanted something *physical* to do, something to keep me *moving*. Something that would make me so tired every day that I wouldn't be able to think. Something to keep us all together – I don't know. But I had to do it right away.'

She looked up at me for a moment, but I didn't say anything. What could I say?

'The last time I saw David we had a stupid argument,' she said. 'We fought, and the next time I hear about him he's … well … I regret how we ended things. *Obviously* I regret how we ended things.'

So that's it: she feels guilty. How horrible for her. But that was only the half of it.

'Also … during the argument I told him to go jump off a cliff. Just like that: "Go jump off a cliff." I know everybody says things like that in the heat of an argument, but it was the *last thing* I said to him. The next thing I hear, he's gone and done just that. I don't like that sort of coincidence. I think that's what Mary meant when she said I had hurt him. I told her about it. I know she only said it out of fear, but what if it really did upset him that I said that? It might be a silly thing to think about, but I can never be truly sure now because he is no longer here to ask.'

Again, I didn't say anything; I just let her talk. At least I understand now why she's been acting the way she has. I think. It's difficult to picture the inner workings of an Alice mind. It's typical of her not to have said anything about how much she's been affected by it.

As for myself, today I feel more depressed than frightened. It's like I'm simply going through the dull motions of finishing the walk, because then – what? I'm done with it? I can wash my hands of it? Hardly. With Yvonne and Mary gone, things will never be the same again. But, I suppose, tonight I'll feel differently; when it gets dark, the terrible fear will come flooding in again.

Alice has just got back – she's taken her time. There was no sign of Mary, or anything else, at the hut, so it's time to pack up and go. It's about 9.5 km to the next hut – Narcissus – and there's a radio there for people to contact the ferry at Cynthia Bay. We assume the ferry won't be running, but someone might still answer us. If not, Alice wants to try and push on and cover as much ground as we can today, so we can get back to civilisation as early as possible tomorrow. No complaints here. I'm just glad Alice wants to get to the end of this terrible track as quickly as I do.

It isn't snowing today, but it is misty. I can feel the rest of the journey stretching out before us like a great dreamscape. I'm fearful of what we might find in it, but there's no other way out.

Afternoon – Narcissus Hut

We've made it to Narcissus Hut, but we won't be staying very long. Naturally we pounced on the ferry radio straight away but, as we had feared, there was no answer to our call, only static. There seemed to be a fatal inevitability to this. I felt a great sinking in my stomach, and knew a hopelessness I have not yet encountered in this nightmare. The track really has been completely shut down this week, and woe betide anyone stupid enough to walk on it. There's now nothing left to do but walk our way out. We're going to rest here for a bit (I can write down the rest of the day's diary), then we'll have one last go on the radio. I'm not holding out any hope, but I guess you never know. Then we'll push on for the last hut at Echo Point.

It feels like a lot has happened today but, on thinking it over, not much has; it just feels that way. I'm very tired, even though the walk was over flat ground and a lot of it on duckboards. The worry I've felt ever since Yvonne vanished has left me drained and on edge.

After 3.5 km through forest, we crossed Stony Creek and continued south along the eastern edge of the Bowling Green – it's flat and green – then walked another 1.7 km until we reached the junction for the track leading to Pine Valley and Pine Valley Hut. Ignoring this, we kept on for a further 2.7 km through the gloom of more forest until we came to another great open space – this time a plain of buttongrass. There's a 400 m duckboard walk spanning this boggy section, and we had a misty view of snow-covered Mount Olympus (1,449 m).

As we were coming to the end of this section, close to a suspension bridge that crosses the Narcissus River, we stopped for a few minutes to get our breath back, and I saw I'd been right to be apprehensive about what the track might still have in store for us. Looking back the way we'd come, we saw someone in the distance making their way along the track towards us. We wondered if it could possibly be Mary so, just in case, we thought we'd better stop and let them catch us up. But it was a terrible nerve-racking wait I was forced to endure. Given what we've already experienced, the approaching figure could have been anything. If it hadn't been for the possibility that it might be Mary, I couldn't have even contemplated staying still like that. Alice was as hard to read as ever, but I think she was feeling the same way. Only the thought of Mary or, by some far-flung chance, Yvonne, could have kept us standing there a moment longer than necessary. What might we be letting catch us up?

So we waited and waited – and waited. Although we could clearly see whomever it was apparently walking towards us, they weren't actually coming any closer. I wondered if it could have been some sort of optical illusion, as there was a slight mist in the air. Eventually it just became too strange and, throwing caution to the wind, we set off to meet them. But we never found out who it was because they suddenly vanished. I looked up from the track to see how far we had to go to get to the spot, and they simply weren't there anymore. A familiar cold tingling sensation crept over me when we realised what had happened. It was more than enough for me to want us to be on our way again but, as always, it was Alice who was thinking the most clearly – unfortunately. She decided we should at least retrace our steps through the buttongrass to the beginning of the forested area in case the stranger had had an accident and come off the duckboards somewhere. There might also be a dip in the track that wasn't noticeable from where we were standing. Neither of us could remember there being anything like this when we were walking through, but in our hurry we might not have noticed. And perhaps it was more that Alice 'reasoned' we should go back, rather than 'decided', as she seemed as happy to dawdle over actually going back as I was.

Eventually we managed to pull ourselves together. Alice was right; we had to make sure it wasn't just someone who'd gotten into trouble on the track and needed our help. At least, that was what I kept telling myself. But when we got to the spot where we thought we'd seen them, there was no sign of anyone. Nor was there anything

on either side of the track, nor footprints in the snow, besides our own. We quickly gave up and went back to the suspension bridge and crossed over it – one at a time as the sign there instructed. Ordinarily, I probably would have found this a little hair-raising, but my mind was on other things just then – it was a relief to start crossing over it.

I think we did all that we could have been expected to do in looking for that person. There was just no one there. It seems to have merely been another way we've been delayed and kept on this track. I want to get out of here so badly.

From the other side of the Narcissus River we continued along for another 1.2 km – the map tells me we were following close to the river bank even though we couldn't always see it through the trees – until we arrived at Narcissus Hut. This one sleeps twenty-eight people and is the most rundown one we've seen so far. But, as I've said, we aren't going to stay here much longer.

Evening – between Byron Gap Junction and Lake St Clair

I am alone. What I feared has happened. Alice has gone. As with the others, I have no idea what happened to her. It suddenly feels like I'm only writing all this down for the police to find later.

With that morbid thought, I shall try to put down everything that happened this afternoon. We tried the radio again at Narcissus, but there was nothing but static coming from the speaker. Then, after a few moments, there was a louder than usual burst of this static or interference, but still no response. At least, so it seemed to me at the time. Now I'm not completely sure, because Alice jumped up and swore like a spooked cat. I've never seen her look so frightened, and she must have been in a few hairy situations climbing all those cliff faces and other things she's done over the years. I was never in those situations with her, of course, but I at least know she's not normally one for showing what she's feeling. Just then her mask slipped, her emotional defences came down, and it made the hairs stand up on my neck again.

She said: 'Did you hear that? Did you hear it?'

'Hear what?' I said, looking all around me.

'Listen!'

She turned up the volume on the radio and listened closely, apprehensively.

After a while the radio spat out another distorted glitch, which I suppose could have been speech, but it really didn't sound like anything to me.

'Oh, no,' she whispered.

I almost didn't hear her, and she had turned very pale, like the snow.

'What?' I said. 'What is it?'

'We have to go now. Right now.' And she started pulling on her pack.

I knew there was no point arguing, so instead I packed up my own pack and strapped myself into it, experiencing the familiar sensation of being pulled backwards under its weight. This close to the end of the walk it should have become lighter because there's less food, but I can't say I've noticed any difference.

When I'd finished, Alice was already waiting outside.

'What's wrong?' I said again as we headed off at a fast walk towards the Lake Marion track junction. With such an overcast sky above us it was already starting to get dark.

Alice didn't answer. In fact, I had to ask another two times before she responded at all.

'We have to keep moving,' she said. 'I want to get to the finish tonight.'

'But it's another fifteen kilometres,' I said, amazed. 'More than fifteen. It'll be completely dark before we get anywhere near Cynthia Bay.'

'So ... we'll just walk in the dark.'

'Through the snow and ice? What's really going on, Alice? What's wrong?'

There was a pause before she said, 'Didn't you hear it on the radio? It was *David* – I'm sure of it. It was David's voice speaking on the radio.'

I almost stopped walking for a second, but Alice was hurrying on faster than ever.

'But it couldn't have been,' I said, now actually struggling to keep up with her – it was hard going over the slippery ground. 'How could it be David's voice? I didn't hear anything.'

Was she imagining things, or could she hear something I couldn't? Maybe my senses *are* failing me. How can I hope to survive this if I can't trust my own ears?

At about this time we started to cross the swampland of the Hamilton Creek Plain, via a long wooden walkway. It was hard to hear what she was saying now because the walkway was so narrow and she was in front. Nor could I turn around to see if anyone was coming up behind us.

'I don't know,' she said. 'Perhaps Mary was right. Maybe Yvonne *did* bring him back somehow. Or maybe he has been with us all the time, and has only now been able to make his presence felt. He has taken the others and now he's coming for me. I *have* to get to the end of the track.'

I couldn't believe what I was hearing. Not from Alice.

'But ... but – Alice, will you stop! I can't talk to you like this.'

Reluctantly she came to a halt and shuffled around on the spot in order to face me.

'Now,' I said, 'even if that were true, why would he take *any* of us? So you blurted out something you regret; we've all done that.'

'You don't understand, Jane. I killed him.' She spoke the words quietly but clearly. 'You can't ...' She sighed. 'We were arguing over Mary. She was in love with him. I couldn't ... I told him – I mean, I didn't mean it; I was just angry – I told him to go and ... well, you know ... But I never thought for one moment he would actually do it.'

'You think he committed suicide?!' I said. 'It wasn't just an accident?'

'I don't know. I don't know at all. But I shouldn't have confided in Mary – she came over all ... superstitious about it. That was stupid of me. And now she's gone.'

After trying to offer you up as a sacrifice, I thought.

'And it should be idiotic to even entertain the idea, but I heard him on that radio, Jane. I heard his voice and he said my name! He wants me, and all I can think about is getting to the end of this horrible track before ... Oh, come on, we've got to keep moving!'

But this doesn't make any sense. Why would Alice be angry at David for Mary being in love with him? Had David led her on? But if so, what was wrong with that? Or did he not return her love? Is that what had upset Alice? And how could anything she might have said about it make him want to kill himself? What was there for him to feel guilty over? There was no time to ask about any of this, however, even if Alice had been willing to be forthcoming about it; she was moving far too quickly. And it was getting darker.

We were now coming to the end of the Hamilton Creek Plain and I was starting to slow down after trying to keep up with Alice for so long. I put on another burst of speed and slipped, falling hard on my chest and causing it to sting and tingle with shock. When I looked up I saw Alice hadn't stopped.

'I can't stop now,' she called. 'You'll have to catch me up. You'll be all right; he won't do anything to you. But I have to go. I'll see you along the track, or at the end. We'll talk then.'

She marched away.

I don't think I blame Alice for doing this. It wasn't something I was happy about – being left on my own like that – but it wasn't the sort of thing she'd normally do. Like me, she's just scared, but, being Alice, she has trouble showing it properly. I think she really does believe David is after her but, whether he is or isn't, he's as much in her mind as he is along the track. And you can't run away from your mind. But if she really does think I'll be safe from him, how does she explain what has happened to Yvonne and Mary?

So now I'm alone, and frightened beyond my ability to accurately describe what I'm feeling. There is something malign here on the track with me, but I can't make up my mind what it is. I personally find it very hard to believe that it can be the spirit of David, but I don't know. Mary and Alice were convinced. I just don't know, and I don't think I want to know.

I had no choice but to carry on by myself. Moving south-east, I entered a thick forest and soon came to a junction leading to Byron Gap and the Cuvier Valley. There was no sign of Alice, with little snow to capture her footprints. But then, about twenty to thirty minutes on from there, I found her pack lying in the middle of the track. There was nothing to say where she'd gone – no trace that I could detect. The ground was littered with rotting moss-covered branches, logs and exposed roots, and I was surrounded by tall trees. Here the track was only marked by the odd metal stake with an orange marker attached to it. I wondered if she might have needed to go to the toilet, and had gone off into the bush, leaving her pack there so I wouldn't walk past her. But I was too frightened to call out and, ironically, hearing the sound of my own voice would have made

me feel more alone. Plus I find it hard to believe Alice would have stopped for anything, given her state of mind, even if she was busting to go. Perhaps, then, she had simply dumped her pack in order to travel faster.

So what was I to do? Should I wait to see if she emerged from the bushes? Should I keep going? What about her pack?

At last I decided to try calling out. What did it matter? After all the things I've witnessed, it was pointless to think I could actually hide myself from whatever it is that's been following us. And I flatter myself that it takes a brave person to willingly break the silence to prove the assertion, to be a physical witness at my own unveiling, even if I do suspect I was never truly hidden in the first place.

I called out Alice's name several times, but the forest remained silent all around me.

I really was on my own now.

I struggled on for a bit longer carrying Alice's pack, but it was just too hard going with the extra weight. I was tired, and by now it was really starting to get dark, being amongst all these trees, so I've made camp right here in the forest (it's mostly myrtle trees, I think). Also, I feel I should stay in the area in case Alice is still here somewhere – even though logic tells me she's gone like the rest. Tomorrow I'll leave her pack behind and go right through to the end of the walk. I don't think I can be that far from reaching the shore of Lake St Clair now; then all I have to do is follow it to Cynthia Bay. That's 8, 9 or 10 km left to do. That's not so bad. It's the waiting to be on my way again that's really getting to me. And I'm not looking forward to tonight when the light disappears completely.

I pitched the tent a little way off the track in as hidden a place as I could find. This wasn't easy to do in the near dark, especially when I'm tired and expecting to be set upon at any moment. I thought about having a rest and something to eat and then maybe trying to walk in the dark with my head torch after all, even if it meant slipping in the snow a lot, but I've given the idea up. It was frightening enough for me to walk that last bit of track on my own while it was still light. My heart was thumping the whole way, and I kept stopping to turn around, thinking I could hear more footsteps, or something moving through the forest on either side of me. I don't think I could do that in the real dark of night. I'd feel like I was being followed every step of the way. And what's worse, I probably would be.

Of course, I still feel very exposed here. Between cooking and writing, with my torch going I must look a bit like a Chinese lantern. But at least it prevents me from seeing the things I imagine to be out there in the dark. And, whatever it is, it won't need light to find me.

A little later

I have just discovered that I have no spare batteries for my torches! I must have left them in Yvonne's pack when it was my turn to carry the tent. Alice has some, but they are the wrong size, and I can't find her torches. I've been using mine more than I anticipated on this trip; I hope they will last.

Night

The footsteps have come again. Whatever it is has found me.

I was lying here, unable to sleep, when I heard the first of them off in the distance. It was the sound of twigs snapping underfoot, and boot falls on the tree roots. Although I couldn't be certain that that's what they were at that point, I became more terrified than I've ever been, as the sound drew nearer and nearer, until I could no longer fool myself that it was merely the wind or an animal. They were the sounds made by a human being, but one I knew wouldn't be there. I think I was shaking, though I didn't realise it at the time, as they slowly walked up to the tent, paused just outside, and then just as slowly moved away again. The rational part of my mind reminds me that nothing has ever come with the appearance of these steps – nothing has ever happened when they walk – but there's always a first time; there's always the unexpected. And it wasn't long after a visitation of these footsteps, or of something seeming to follow us, that the others vanished. It's hard to be rational sitting here in the dark – on my own – with these things happening. Or perhaps it's easy, because if I don't keep it together it'll be the end of everything, and I won't have to worry then. Making myself write all this down is helping a little. I continue to record the facts and figures from the guidebook as best as I can, as I find it reassuring. It's something solid and real and tested; the opposite of whatever is happening to me now.

Why did Alice have to say such a thing to David – *Go jump off a cliff*? I find it hard to believe she would ever say – actually, no. No, I can believe it, especially if she was in the middle of an argument. But she wouldn't have really meant it; David would have known that. There's nothing to say that he died of anything other than an accident. How could she think she was responsible for his death? Mind you, those Egyptian spells are supposed to work by the power of words, aren't they? Can mere words really be that powerful? I don't know. It seems impossible.

I've got Yvonne's *Book of the Dead* with me now. I'm keeping it, whether it's had anything to do with anything or not, because the spells have become a strange sort of comfort to me, like they're something natural when we've been experiencing so much that's unnatural. It's almost become like a shield to me; if it *has* caused harm, maybe it can ward it off as well.

So – what else? I need to keep writing. What is my own preferred method of dying, if I had the choice? No, it's not the most pleasant of things to be thinking about, but it's something to write, and it's important to me not to leave anything out of this record. I've known for a long time what it would be, and it fills me with a prophetic sense of dread to write it down, but – if I had to choose – it would be to simply walk away from everything and never be heard from again. Just disappear. The question is is it really going to happen to me now? It seems to have been what happened to the others. And what does 'just disappearing' actually mean? I've always thought of it from everyone else's point of view. The point of view that is full of the mystery, and even the romance, of a disappearance. But what really is the reality of it all? I suppose it's like asking what the reality of being asleep is. I don't know, nor can I even fathom it.

I can hear animals outside – rustling in the trees and moving about, coming near the tent. But I'm not afraid of them. I still haven't actually seen any, apart from a couple of birds flying overhead; I've only heard them a few times in the night when we've been in the tents. I wonder if they run away when 'it' walks through the forest. Is that how it moves? It walks? Maybe the animals don't notice it. Maybe it's not there at all and I'm just crazy. Maybe I've killed the others but I don't know it. Anything seems possible. I might have fallen asleep in the car on the way to the start of the track. I hope not – I don't want to have to do the walk all over again!

We set off on this journey because of our feelings for David. It seems to have turned out to be nothing but one long funeral march after all.

DAY EIGHT

Morning

At least, it's light outside – I don't know what the time is.

And I'm still here.

Nothing else happened during the night – I didn't hear the footsteps again – and, now that the sun has come up, some of my fears have melted away. But only some of them; the forest around me casts long shadows. I don't know how I managed to fall asleep, but eventually I must have.

I'm going to leave Alice's pack here under a tree and tie one of her brighter tops to a branch to mark its position. I've decided to continue carrying my own pack, even though it would probably make more sense to leave it behind so I can move faster. No doubt they'll be collected by the searchers or someone after I've raised the alarm – or after Liz does – but I feel like it isn't enough to only get myself out of this horrible park; I need to know I'm not leaving any of my stuff behind as well. It's like – yes, it's like my stuff is … not a part of me, exactly … but something similar, something that's just as vulnerable, and I can't bear to think of it being left behind. A little like my grave goods, I suppose.

It can't be much further before I reach the shore of Lake St Clair; then it's only a few kilometres along its bank until I reach Echo Point Hut. There's supposed to be a jetty there – I *might* even find people. But, if not, there's just the final 10 km straight on to the visitor centre at Cynthia Bay – all along a flat path. And there, safety. I know I can make it in a day.

Before I fell asleep last night, I was going over one of the spells Yvonne had read out: 'Spell for not permitting a man's heart to be taken from him in the realm of the dead'. Going over and over it. Particularly the bit where it says:

> He sends out his heart which controls his body, his
> heart is announced to the gods, for David's heart is his
> own, he has power over it … He himself has power
> over his members, his heart obeys him …

Did we, somehow, possess David's heart, just by loving him, each in our way – whatever metaphor you think that represents? The heart kept popping up in the spells. Have they enabled him to come back to look for it? Does that mean he loves us? Or hates us? Alice seemed to think he hated her. Or is whatever the heart represents important to all dead people? Are we disturbing his rest by possessing it? Is it because we haven't been able to talk about him, to let him go? Or does it have nothing to do with what's happening to us? What's happening to me!

Well, I'm packed and ready to go. It's time to get out of here.

I'm so near the end, yet must pass through so much more. Whatever it is that's on the track with me, there's nothing I can do about it, any more than Yvonne, Mary and Alice could. We've all been trying to run from it in one way or another for most of this walk, but I now know there's nowhere to go, nowhere to hide. For all I know, I won't be safe at the visitor centre either, even surrounded by people. It's odd, given the circumstances, but I feel strange about the idea of being around people again – at least a lot of people. I've grown accustomed to them not being here. If 'it' wants to take me like the others, then I suppose it will. And is 'it' David? If it was David as I knew him when he was alive I'd have said no, absolutely not, but if it's possible to survive the death of your body, then who knows how that may change someone? *The Book of the Dead* paints rather a strange picture of the afterlife. And I suppose it depends on how David was really feeling about Alice when he died.

I can't say I'm ready for it, but here I go: my last day on the track – for good or bad.

Later – Echo Point Hut

I've made it to Echo Point Hut. The going wasn't difficult. All is well.

The hut is pretty basic and small, sleeping eight people. I think it used to be painted red at some point, at least the front of it was, but it's now mostly worn off. It's sat in a little dark clearing close to the lake shore. I think the red might have been to make it visible from the lake. There's another jetty here for the ferry. It makes me think of the 'Spell for not letting David be ferried over to the East'. According to *The Book of the Dead*, you don't want that particular ferryman to turn up.

It still feels very lonely and desperate out here, despite knowing how close I am to the visitor centre. The guidebook says it'll take three hours to get there. I'll be on my way again soon.

Letter to the Parks and Reserves Manager from the Ranger in Charge of the Overland Track (Cradle Mountain – Lake St Clair National Park)

Strictly confidential

Dear ▆▆▆▆▆▆▆▆▆▆▆▆,

Another four walkers have disappeared on the Overland Track. These are the first since we began closing it for the week-long period in which the activity and other disappearances have occurred. This brings the number of unexplained disappearances up to nine.

The walkers have been identified as Alice Northrop, 31; Jane Hill, 30; Mary Bell, 30; and Yvonne Fenn, 31.

The alarm was raised by Liz Gore, a friend of the group, on the ▆th when they failed to arrive at the Lake St Clair visitor centre, having set out from Cradle Mountain eight days earlier. They were two days overdue at this point.

Assisted by Ms Gore, the group had managed to sneak onto the track while it was closed. Apparently they had been unable to acquire four walking permits at short notice, so had decided to do the track during the closure, and thus avoid paying the track fees at the same time.

The closure period over, a search party was immediately sent out from the Lake St Clair end of the track, on foot and by helicopter. A hiking pack belonging to Jane Hill was found on the track approximately half a kilometre from the Echo Point promontory. As in the previous incidents, neither the pack nor the surrounding area showed signs of violence. Inside the pack was found a journal kept by Ms Hill, which documents the group's day-to-day progress. As you are aware, it has been theorised that the unnerving incidents reported to us by some of the park rangers may be connected with the disappearance of the previous walkers. This journal would seem to support that idea, and it gives us a firsthand account of the prolonged physiological and psychological effects felt by those experiencing this phenomenon. That is, if their experience *was* similar to the previous walkers. The journal does not, however, appear to shed any new light on the root cause of it all. On the contrary, it only adds to the mystery and leaves us with more questions. It describes how the group was subjected to a frightening succession of persecutions and disappearances as they tried to flee the track but, given their current frame of mind (they had recently suffered the loss of a close friend), how much of what they experienced, or what the writer thought they experienced, can be attributed to their own nervous imagination is hard to say. Are all these people simply going 'track crazy'? The journal also gave the location of the other three abandoned hiking packs, which made their recovery easier.

The journal makes reference to something following the group, and to mysterious footsteps heard outside the huts and their tents during the night – very like the reports given by the rangers. Their attempts to locate the source of these noises proved unsuccessful; nor could we find evidence of anyone other than the four women on the track. As with the previous disappearances, no bodies have been found, and snowfall has obliterated any tracks – and no PLB was activated, as they weren't carrying one. The journal also talks of photographs that the women thought might contain an image of their pursuer. But, on reviewing the contents of all the devices that were recovered, no conclusive images could be found. The 'figure' in question may simply be a part of the landscape.

The group made repeated attempts to radio for help, but were either unable to gain access to the rangers' rooms or, in the case of Narcissus Hut, they simply could not get through to anybody. This – unfortunately – was probably due to some of the staff on duty at Lake St Clair continuing to refuse to monitor the radios during the period of activity, because of the distressing calls and noises that have been heard coming over the channel. As I have mentioned to you on previous occasions, when investigated these sounds seem to have no point of origin.

Interestingly, the party of women came to believe that the presence they perceived was somebody they knew – a recently deceased man named David Holt. In fact, in the next of the packs to be discovered, we found this curious, appartently hastily writen, letter from Alice Northrop addressed to the other three. It appears they had no knowledge of its existence.

It reads:

> To my dear friend Jane
> (and also to Mary and Yvonne, wherever you may be),
>
> I am writing this note in the event that something
> happens to me on this walk and I do not see you again.

I do not understand what has been happening to us but, whatever it is, I wish to leave behind me this confession.

First of all, I am so very sorry for dragging you all into this mess. I wasn't quite honest about why I wanted to do the walk, and if it wasn't for my selfishness none of you would be here. I know David's death hit us all hard, but the grief and the guilt of it was crushing me more than I could stand. I desperately needed to be doing something physical and mindless to drive out the horrible negative thoughts that were plaguing my mind. When I go walking for any length of time my mind goes blank; I am only thinking of where to place my next step. Doing a long bushwalk seemed perfect; it would be a whole six days of walking, and no other bad news would be able to reach me – I wouldn't have been able to cope with anything else going wrong. Here I could push all those unbidden thoughts from my mind. I would no longer have to think about David and the fact that we ourselves are all going to die eventually. Or at least the thoughts wouldn't appear with such force; the time would allow them to gradually trickle through my mind, where they could be sifted and sifted into more digestible pieces. I just had to get away. It was like a compulsion, getting worse and worse. It felt almost as if David were pursuing me himself, demanding that I give him – and what had happened to him – my complete attention. I simply wasn't ready to deal with all that so soon. I don't think any of us were, judging by the way we avoided talking about him as we walked. I often wondered what you were all thinking. And perhaps that wasn't right. Maybe we should have opened up about how we were feeling and coping – or not coping. But, to begin with, it was all too much for me, and I simply wasn't able to think straight. It didn't matter that it was the middle of winter and that the rest of you were so inexperienced at bushwalking; I had to go. I had to push all thoughts of David from my mind. I didn't know what else to do. I simply couldn't wait for enough places to become available on the track. So when I saw that it would be closing soon and that no one would be there to stop us sneaking onto it, it seemed like it was meant to be.

But I couldn't walk every waking moment while I was on the track; I wish I could have. So I brought you all along with me. I lied to you when I said David had wanted us to do it together, but it seemed like none of you would have come otherwise. It was selfish, but I wanted someone to talk to and to listen to in the evenings when I couldn't walk anymore and the thoughts might rush back in. Also, there would be safety in numbers. If it wasn't for that, I think I would have gone on my own. Now you know what sort of a person brought you on this trip. Though, in my defence, I think there was something about it being just us, we four women together, with no one else around. And I really did think we would be all right, that I could handle it. But I couldn't, and it was unfair of me to put you all through it. I have let you all down.

I don't know why I picked the Overland Track; it just seemed right somehow. The right number of days, the right distance away from the world, and I admit saving some money did appeal to me, in the same way that not buying the personal locator beacon did when I saw how expensive they are. It just seemed so unnecessary. I thought we would be all right. I would be with you, and I have done lots of things like this before, many of them alone, and have never needed one. We would all be together if anything went wrong. When Yvonne disappeared, I really thought I could handle the situation. Then, when Mary went, I still thought that if only I could get us to the end of the track they would both turn up and there would be no need for anyone to find out that we had ever been there. That's why I wasn't keen on breaking into the rangers' room. To damage something would have been the point of no return, and would have meant that I had failed to look after you all, when it was me who had insisted on you coming along. Several times now I have been terrified on this track, but I needed to face that fear where I could. I needed to stay in control and to finish what I had planned for us; otherwise the fear that I could see creeping up on you and Mary would have got me too, and I would have been of no use to anybody. I had to force myself to go outside to look for a rational explanation to those footsteps. But it was all nonsense – I wasn't in control of myself; I was just pretending that I could cope with it all. And now we are just running from whatever is happening to us.

When I last saw David, we had an argument. It ended with me telling him to go and throw himself off a cliff – not to actually kill himself – it was just a figure of speech because I was so furious. But it was the last thing I said to him. Then not long after this confrontation he really did fall from a cliff and die! Now that Mary has gone and we may never see her again, I can admit that the argument was over her, over David's inability to return the feelings she had for him. I know we all loved him, and he cared for us, but he loved me more – we were keeping it a secret so as not to hurt Mary – and he would have done anything for me, I am sure of it. So when I effectively told him to go and kill himself, maybe he did somehow. He was being so blasé about Mary's feelings that I got angry with him and stormed off. I really felt for her because of that. When he saw how much he had upset me, maybe he later regretted the way he had acted, and went and did what I had said. I mean who really knows what's in someone else's mind?

But I have another reason for thinking myself guilty, and it is this that I wish to confess to. Perhaps, as you read this, my conscience is now at rest, but my guilt is certain. Just before we got into our argument, I lent David one of my climbing ropes for his trip. A section of this had become frayed and needed to be removed to make the rope safe to use. When we got into the fight I forgot all about it. When I remembered again it was too late; he had left for his climbing trip. I tried to get him on his phone, but he must have been out of range by then. Is this how he died? Because of my rope? I haven't been brave enough to find out what sort of condition it was in when his body was recovered. Did he notice the damage before he used it? It was his responsibility to check his equipment, but there is no doubt I failed him. Or was he punishing me by not replying to the texts I sent him because I had gotten angry with him? He knew I would be worrying about him.

For what it is worth now, I am sorry for what I have done. If my faulty gear and, above all, my failure to mention the fault, was responsible for David's death, then perhaps I deserve to disappear too. I do not understand what is happening to us on this track; it seems to defy explanation. Now, possibly, I will have no need of any explanation, for it may have come for me too.

Alice

The closing and vacating of the track for the week in question was thought to be an adequate solution to the problem, but this latest incident highlights the need for more and continued diligence in securing its access points. We know the track does pose a real danger to the public – whatever its cause – but it is difficult to see what more can be done to keep people off it during this time. That is, short of actually telling the public that we believe there is something sinister and unexplainable stalking the track. Though that's just as likely to encourage more people to sneak onto it as it is to keep them away, and our job will be made even harder. So far, none of our rangers have gone missing – they have merely been frightened by the phenomena – but there is no reason to believe that they are immune to whatever is happening. I believe what they tell me, and the disquiet caused by these incidents alone is enough to make their work intolerable during the closure. I therefore continue to back them in their refusal to go onto the track during this period. I even allowed them to place a little memorial plaque in the forest near Pelion Gap, in the hope of appeasing the spirit of any walker or ranger who died on the track and who might be causing the phenomena. But, of course, it had no effect.

We might look into the viability of installing surveillance cameras at the hut sites, etc., but they would need to have a real-time link with the outside to be of any use. The question is would these suffer from the same interference problems as the radios? And if they did pick up images of people who aren't supposed to be there, who would be prepared to walk in and fetch them out? And what would be the point, as the people in question would be in the process of walking out anyway? We would have to send in a helicopter and, depending on where on the track they might be, it could take some considerable time to locate them. Can we justify that sort of expense? Questions would be asked, and we would be forced to admit that we thought they were in danger from something that seems to be very much supernatural in nature.

As has previously been discussed, I have no doubt that this sort of talk would lead to ridicule and the track perhaps being closed down altogether. As per your instructions, therefore, I did not give the journal to the police when I handed over the women's packs. It would only serve to invite media speculation and sensation. I believe we can continue to rely on the silence of the park staff for this same reason. But the journal may be useful evidence, should anyone take it into their head to think that we had anything to do with the disappearances. We can always say it was 'found' sometime later if this becomes necessary. But it is not in our interests to frighten people off the track with ghostly tales of walkers being 'taken' – even if we really have no idea what is happening to them.

I await any comments or instructions you may have in this matter.

Yours,

███████████

The End

www.ingramcontent.com/pod-product-compliance
Lightning Source LLC
Chambersburg PA
CBHW010449100726
47904CB00008B/2542